Said the Fly

By Laurie Taylor

Traveling Light Press
Walnut Creek, California

Said the Fly

By Laurie Taylor

Published by

Traveling Light Press

633 New Seabury Ct.

Walnut Creek, CA 94598

Dedicated to my mother, who, among other things, taught me to read.

Author's Note

As anyone well versed in geography will surely know, there is no island in the *Canarias* by the name of La Sirena. If you have visited that part of the world, you might identify the places that inspired this story. If you have never been to the islands, you may recognize your own lost paradise, wherever that may be. All characters and events are purely fictional, with exception of the Tambovskaya-Malyshevkaya gang, Russian mobsters who unfortunately do exist. Some of their leaders were captured in 2008, in Spain, while escaping the winter weather of Berlin and St. Petersburg.

1

La mosca. The fly, evident to my naked eye as a *Calliphora*, or, as it is commonly known, a blowfly, was buzzing loudly and throwing itself angrily against its paper prison, a super-sized soda cup with a snap-on lid.

There I was at the scene of the crime, still in my silk bathrobe, my wavy dark hair loose but minimally under control, tucked behind my ears. Chief Inspector Ballero and I were sitting on the top of the stone steps leading down to the water. He chain-smoked during his interrogation, occasionally casting distracted glances at the noisy drink cup. Three of his team, two in Guardia Civil uniform, and one in an outfit that looked as though he planned on attending Mass instead of a murder scene, were examining Esmeralda and the beach for evidence.

It was Sunday morning and way too early for anyone but a fisherman to be up and moving about—a fisherman or Udo, the German owner of the beach bar Café Sport, that supplied the first coffee of the day. While sweeping the entrance to his bar, Udo had spotted me sitting alone on the steps, waiting for the police.

"It's Esmeralda," I told him, "and she's dead. Someone has killed her." After walking over for a quick, close look, he kept me company until the authorities arrived. "Fucking unbelievable," he said, and after that we just sat there together in a comfortable silence.

It was chilly and I clutched the collar of my robe tightly around my throat. The newly risen sun had yet to clear the towering cliffs sheltering the southwestern harbor town. We would remain in shade for at least another half hour before the sun we shared with the African coast dazzled above us. The water was slate blue, reflecting little of the suffused dawn sky.

Udo seemed genuinely upset about Esmeralda, although I knew from previous conversations with him that there had been no love lost between these two neighbors. He rolled a cigarette from a pack of *American Spirit* and I noticed his hands were trembling. I didn't think it was just from the chill in the air. "Poor, poor girl," he said finally.

Café Sport was next door to Esmeralda's nightclub, and on the ground floor of our holiday apartment building. Her mother was Udo's landlady as well as ours. In Udo's presence, the shock of my discovery felt more real. Though we weren't close friends, I was grateful for his company on the stairs next to me: his long arms wrapped around his knees pulled up close to his chest, a cigarette burning into ash between his fingers. I'd never seen him outside of the murky interior of the Café Sport. He looked even paler and more dissipated in the unforgiving daylight. I noticed faint tracks of acne scarring behind his five o'clock shadow. We sat like two birds on a line waiting for something to happen.

After what had seemed forever, a police car pulled up, and parked to deliberately block off the narrow road. Four men got out and hurried passed us down the stairs to the beach and over to the corpse. In a few minutes, the tallest one turned back and came over to speak with us.

I'd never been a witness at a murder scene. I thought about how simple some things remained in the far corners of the world. If we were on a beach in my home state of California, under these circumstances the road would have been cordoned off with a large forensic team swarming around the area, Udo and I might already have been taken down to the police station for questioning.

Instead, Ballero had just plunked himself down on one of the stairs above us and lit a cigarette. He nodded to Udo and then addressed me in Spanish, in a raspy voice: "You are the lady that called the station and reported the body?" I just answered, *"Si."* I was acutely aware of the fly's buzzing growing louder and more insistent.

"¿Y esto qué, es esto?" He frowned at the cup.

All I'd thought about earlier, once I'd understood that Esmeralda was dead—and had been for some time—was how to trap the fly crawling on the knife sticking out from her back. The weapon was at an oblique angle, leaving the wound exposed under the tear in her blood stained T-shirt, and not entirely plugged by the hilt. It was this small opening that had attracted the fly. When I caught her, she'd been leisurely examining the wound's perimeter, using her feet to measure the optimum depth and moisture zone in which to deposit her eggs.

I didn't mean to disturb the crime scene, but I don't think it looked that way to the Inspector. I guess in the excitement of the moment, it had escaped my mind that all that garbage could contain evidence. That something tossed in there might link someone to the body sprawled just above the high-water line, where the last tide had left an assorted collection of mostly unnatural gifts from the sea.

"Por favor perdona mi error."

I confessed to him that I'd taken the soda cup from the trash can, pried off the plastic lid, shaken out the remaining drops of liquid, discarded the straw, and then held the cup upside down above the wound. I explained how I maneuvered it to startle the fly into flying up into the interior of the cup while I slid on the lid from below, without grazing the rim of the wound or disturbing the knife. This would have been difficult for the average person, but since my area of expertise is necrophageous scavengers, I'd practiced this countless times on pigs, chickens, and other dead mammals, using specimen vials with much narrower openings than the cup, when it wasn't possible or desirable to use a net.

I told the Chief Inspector I was shocked at the sight of Esmeralda's body, and that my thoughts immediately went to her mother, Constanze Therese and Esmeralda's sweet eleven-year-old daughter, Serenella, who now would have neither father nor mother, as Esmeralda was a single parent. What I didn't add was that, although I was feeling these sympathetic emotions, a part of my mind was working on the significance of that fly and its mission.

Maybe it was that my Mexican Spanish was not so lovely to Ballero's ears, or that this was his first murder investigation in over a decade on La Sirena, the smallest Canary Island, a few miles offshore of Western Sahara, but he seemed wary of my account of how I found the corpse. Of course, I knew the fact that I was an American and a *doctora*—a Ph.D in Zoology, not a medical doctor—insulated me somewhat from serious heat. Nevertheless, this paunchy head of local law enforcement was not very happy with me.

He asked twice how I could have recognized from such a distance that it was Esmeralda lying on the beach, when the balcony of our apartment was three stories above the ground, and over forty meters from the black volcanic sand.

I told him that at first she'd simply looked like someone sleeping off a party from the night before, face down, arms overhead. Yet something told me that Esmeralda, my landlady's daughter and the owner of the town's disco, was not just stone drunk and passed out. Something told me even at that distance that she was, well, stone dead.

I explained to Ballero that I'd been trained in the subtle nuances of form, line, and proportion in anatomy, and that I have spent years learning to observe fine details in the structures of insects—mainly flies and beetles— to be able to recognize the differences between species. I find that I can apply these skills to people as well. When talking with someone, my eye is always roving across their composite parts, analyzing the mathematical relationships which make that particular individual exactly who they are.

In many ways, Esmeralda appeared similar to other local young women. Her hair was dark and curly, tipped with gold streaks and tied back with a hair stretchy at the base of her neck. She was wearing a denim mini-skirt and a pale blue Adidas T-shirt. From the balcony her face wasn't visible, but I knew the body on the beach was Esmeralda because of the length of her legs and arms, and how they were just slightly longer than the stockiness of her torso and the ample width of her hips would imply.

"Entonces, Señorita," Ballero addressed me, as he lit his second cigarette and stared intently. "Explain to me exactly what you were doing with that fly."

"Well," I answered slowly, calculating just how specific my explanation of forensic entomology should be. From his initial reaction, I could see that this subject was clearly news to Ballero—which was understandable. A colony of flies, beetles, moths, and tiny parasitic wasps moving to and from a decomposing corpse is a carefully orchestrated *pas-de-deux* between chemistry and time. Each new step is cued by temperature changes and subsequent volatile odors. Before television crime lab shows became so popular, not many homicide police had ever heard of, let alone used, this method of resolving an enigmatic death. I knew for a fact that only a few entomologists on mainland Spain were in this line of research.

Though I'm not a medico-legal practitioner, my area of research is directly related. My best friend, Amy Gardiner, became the first forensic entomologist on the homicide squad of the San Jose Police Department. In graduate school, we had spent many hours together collecting from experimental animal corpses planted in the different ecological environments where police records revealed most murder victims were found outdoors in our region of the state.

During those three years we practically lived in our lab on Subway sandwiches, Diet Cokes, and Reese's Peanut Butter Cups, while we curated and identified thousands of flies.

I revised a genus in the family of an aquatic fly, notably found on 'floaters'—bodies retrieved from water. Amy's project established an electronic data bank of our local species and all relevant ecological data, now used by both FBI and state law enforcement in northern and central California.

I was an expert of sorts in the academic field, but I didn't want to alienate Ballero and ruin my chances of possibly helping to solve Esmeralda's murder. So how I presented myself as well as my credentials was very important.

"First of all, let me apologize for the a..." I hesitated searching for the right word, "... *unauthorized* capture of this fly, but it is almost second nature for me, as this is my line of work, *Señor* Ballero. As you know, a dead body becomes a source of food for many insects after a certain number of hours pass."

Ballero nodded his head as if it were very heavy.

"The body temperature must drop and the decay process progress before a fly will become attracted to it. Normally, this type of fly..." I tapped the paper cup for emphasis, " ... will be the first to arrive. She'll want to lay her eggs in the moist areas to prevent their desiccation—the mouth, the eyes, the nasal and genital cavities—but an open wound is more enticing to her. She'll walk in the wound..." I demonstrated with two fingers moving across my bare knee, "and she will determine with her feet the best place for her children to develop."

For a moment, I was uncomfortably aware that my mimicry of the fly's dance had drawn both men's attention to my bare legs. I hurried on. "I don't know if this fly deposited her eggs. Sometimes the body has decomposed just long enough to attract her, but not enough to induce her to release her eggs. I can later dissect her abdomen to see," I hesitated again, "and with permission, examine the wound."

There was no immediate response from Ballero, so I continued my explanation, trying not to sound like a National Geographic special, but at the same time getting my main points across.

"Depending on the ambient temperature and climatic conditions of the environment where the body has been situated, and also on the local species that are prevalent during that season, a person trained in their biological requirements can understand pretty clearly the probabilities of what could or could not have occurred."

The Chief Inspector now looked more interested.

Udo wrinkled his forehead in concentration, as he could only catch parts of what I was saying in Spanish.

"Time of death, of course, is most important in a murder investigation, but location of the murder, in some circumstances, can be determined as well. For instance, I cannot say for sure at this moment, as I haven't had a chance to examine Esmeralda's body thoroughly, but I already expect there is a good probability that she was not killed here on the beach or in her nightclub, as someone would like you to believe."

Ballero was now looking at me with increasing curiosity. I was waiting for him to ask me why, but he surprised me by asking something all together different.

"Dime, Señorita, you come from *where* in America?"

"I come from California, but I now live in Germany, in Berlin. I am working at the Museum of Natural History in a post-doc position."

"Your Spanish..."

"My mother was Mexican; I grew up bilingual. Now, I'm trying to learn this awful German language," I said smiling and gesturing towards Udo. I was deliberately trying to get on Ballero's good side with a little German-bashing. I figured Udo was used to it, if he even understood.

"And your name?"

"Dr. Epiphany Jerome." I held out my hand as though we were being formally introduced. He took it politely.

"Do you know Dr. Juan Lopez at the *Parque?"* he asked.

My heart skipped. Now here was a personal connection, the best reference I could have from a local authority. Dr. Lopez was the senior scientist at the *Parque Nacional del Valle de Cedro*, the UNESCO World Heritage Site of nature conservation in the central part of the island.

"*¡Si, claro!* I've been up there several times, and we've spoken together. He's a botanist, of course. I learned quite a lot about your endemic plants from him, as well as the insect species that exist only here on La Sirena."

Whatever his connection to Lopez, he was now noticeably more at ease with me. Everyone knew everyone in this small town. My husband and I had been here just short of a month, vacationing from the interminable winter weather of Berlin. I already knew quite a bit about Esmeralda and her family, and even more about Udo and his six years of being an expat German bar owner in Spain. I even knew the Chief Inspector was the brother of Hector Ballero, one of the richest men on the island, though I'd never met either of them before. So it didn't seem strange to me that the three of us sat there so casually, while Ballero postponed going up the hill to tell Constanze Therese, whom he'd probably gone to school with, that her only daughter was dead.

Our conversation, or more accurately, Ballero's questions and our answers, lurched through three languages. Udo, like many of the Germans on the island, had never bothered to learn more Spanish than was strictly necessary for conducting business; his English was fair. Ballero, like many island natives, regarded the influx of winter tourists and the rapid invasion of German-owned properties and businesses, with a combination of resignation and barely disguised resentment. His German was next to nil, his English non-existent. After two years of living in Germany, I understood a lot more German than I could actually speak. I spoke in Spanish to Ballero and translated whenever they hit a language barrier.

We both told Ballero that the techno music coming from the disco had continued until 4:00 a.m. when either Esmeralda or her bartender had closed down the club. Udo, who lived in an apartment above Café Sport, recalled seeing two cars illegally parked on the road. Esmeralda's club attracted the late-night crowd from the twenty or so other bars in the town. They were all within walking distance, so it was rare that anyone drove the narrow street to the club or Café Sport, since there was nowhere to park safely. Esmeralda's mother owned this short strip of converted warehouses as well as our apartment building. The pavement dead-ended and a dirt road carved off into the hill above us and eventually ran past the big split-level *hacienda* where Esmeralda had lived with her mother and her daughter.

Ballero listened closely to what Udo and I could recall about the night before, drawing deeply on his cigarette. His eyes scanned across the volcanic sand to where Esmeralda lay like something washed up from a shipwreck. His broad, rounded shoulders heaved, and I thought I heard him sigh.

I made a decision that I would one day regret. I offered my professional services to help solve Esmeralda's murder.

"*Señor* Ballero, if I can help you in this investigation, I'd be very pleased." Ballero appeared to be intrigued, so I continued, "But I'm wondering do you have a pathologist on the island, or will you use someone on Tenerife?"

Ballero thrust his hand with the cigarette out towards the group of men on the beach. "The man in the suit is our coroner, but yes, the pathologist from Tenerife has been called, and will be arriving on the fast boat at noon."

The 'fast' boat took over three hours to get here and was only scheduled twice daily.

I paused, as I did not yet understand if Ballero was accepting my help. "Could I speak with you and the coroner together, and show you something on the body which I think you'll find extremely important?"

Ballero seemed then to remember Udo's presence. Dismissing him with a curt nod, the policeman lifted his considerable weight from his sitting position, and crushed the cigarette butt under his well-polished shoe. He escorted me down the stairs towards the body. I knew the sun would make its appearance any minute. I was hoping, but seriously doubting, that the coroner had already taken the temperature of the corpse, the air and the ground.

I was wondering too, when Ballero would break the news to Constanze Therese that Serenella's mother was never coming home.

2

When I returned to our apartment, my husband, Mimmo, was having his typical Italian breakfast on the balcony—espresso with two teaspoons of sugar and a cookie. Our little dog, Mostly, sitting at his feet, wagged his tail, frantically happy at the sound of my arrival. Mostly's mother was Jack Russell terrier and his father was of unknown origin; so we named him 'Mostly' as we like to think he is mostly Jack Russell. Although a certain pudginess to his proportions and a wooliness in his fur betrays him as having 'foreign blood,' as the Jack Russell Club of America likes to put it.

I picked Mostly up, hugged him, and told Mimmo that it was Esmeralda's corpse that the blue and yellow ambulance was carrying away from the beach.

"Was ist los?" Mimmo and I generally speak English together, but when he's tired, angry, or in this case, taken by surprise, he reverts to Italian or his second language, German.

"I woke up early and was having my coffee here and I noticed her body at the far end of the beach. I thought at first she was passed out from drinking, but something told me she was dead."

"Madonna!"

"I went down there and saw she had a knife sticking out of her back."

"How did you know she was dead? You didn't try and take out the knife or help her?"

"Of course I didn't take out the knife! Do you think I'm crazy? I tried to take her pulse but she was cold, so I came back up here to use your cell phone and called the police."

I took a deep breath. I was getting unreasonably irritated with Mimmo.

"Udo came out and waited with me until the Chief Inspector—Hector Ballero's brother by the way— and La Guardia Civil and the ambulance came."

"*Mamma mia!* Why didn't you wake me up?"

"I don't know, I guess I was just in shock and I thought it was better to talk with the police alone. There was nothing you could do, and Mostly would have been a nuisance if we'd brought him down there to the beach, and he would have barked and woken up the neighbors if we left him behind."

Mimmo regarded me with one eyebrow raised, and he noticed how Mostly's attention was fixed on the buzzing soda cup in my hand.

"You didn't take a bug off the body, did you, Epiphany? Are you crazy? Yes, you are crazy!" He threw his hands up in the air. "This is not California! You don't know these people. This is murder, not some funny business. I don't want you getting mixed up in this business. In your typical arrogant American way, you think you can just go in wherever you like and fix everyone's problems."

Mimmo's words hit their intended mark and I was silent, thinking about my response. I hated it when my European friends saw me as an American with all the accompanying baggage, some of it stereotype, and some of it closer to the truth than I liked to admit.

"Please, Mimmo, first I need to eat something," I put Mostly back down on the floor, "and then I want to have a look at this fly. Ballero's meeting me at one o'clock at the offices of the *Guardia*, and taking me to the morgue to meet the pathologist, who's coming here on the fast boat from Tenerife. I do know something about what I am doing, and I think I can help them get to the truth of what happened."

I sat down opposite him at the little patio table.

"I know you want to protect me, but I really need to do this. I've always envied Amy getting to do real forensic police work while I just run cladistics software and look for genetic markers in my beetles and flies. Yeah, I'm being selfish because being on this little island in the middle of this ocean gives me an opportunity I might not otherwise have in some big city... I don't find dead bodies every day..."

I paused to give emphasis to the drama warranted by this last observation, "But also, I feel I owe it to Serenella and Constanze Therese to help find

Esmeralda's murderer. She's not just a *body*. I know this person. I know this family. I don't know how I'm going to be able to look at them without breaking into tears!"

Mimmo was softening. I tried one last thing. "You can come with me, if you want. We can leave Mostly downstairs with Udo. You know he likes Udo, because he gives him scraps of *Wurst* whenever we're in the Sport." Mimmo relented, smoked a Fortuna, and watched the police, who were still milling around on the beach. I placed the cup in the freezer to kill the fly while I made my breakfast.

After eating, I took the fly out from the freezer to thaw, so I could manipulate it without damage. I showered, blow-dried my hair, and put on a dress that made me look slightly more professional than my normal choice: T-shirt and cargo pants.

Mimmo stayed with Mostly on the balcony, distractedly reading a two-day-old copy of *La Repubblica*, while keeping one eye on the action on the beach.

My field microscope was set up on a freestanding kitchen counter attached to the wall, above one of the few electrical outlets in the apartment. Next to the counter, there was a small east-facing window, overlooking the dirt road leading up towards Constanze Therese's home. I could see Ballero's police car was still parked up there.

I pinned the fly through its dorsum and placed the pin in a small ball of clay so that I could easily rotate the fly under the lens of my scope, while methodically checking it for all taxonomic characters, even though I already knew it was a *Calliphora vicinia*:

> *Blue abdomen and black head with red to yellow bucca. Thorax: black to dark blue-green. Coated with fine hairs and grayish powder lending it a silver appearance. Faint, longitudinal stripes on dorsal surface.*

I placed the fly in a dissecting pan filled with 70‰ alcohol solution. With two very fine needles attached to toothpicks, I was able to remove the cuticle and guts that protected her ovary. I could see from the state of her distended abdomen and organs, and her oviaroles—one egg-packed and the other empty—that I had indeed interrupted Madam Fly's egg laying. I felt sure I'd find eggs in the knife wound.

I prepared the fly's body and her ovary for archival evidence, labeling them and making relevant notations for a police report. The routine details of this delicate work had a soothing effect on my nerves. I felt more like myself again, less shaken by the disturbing sight of Esmeralda dead on the beach.

"Mimmo," I called to my husband on the balcony, "It's almost eleven o'clock. I'm going to the Internet place. Can you meet me there after you take Mostly to Café Sport?"

I packed the evidence into my backpack, and hurried out the door.

* * *

Uno Mundo was more than just your average Internet café. Its German owners had had the brilliant idea of playing world music nonstop in a comfortable, colorful ambiance and displaying the CDs around the front desk for sale. If one of them interested a customer, they would play it for you while you checked your email or browsed the web.

It was my favorite place to be in town. I often took my laptop there to use their wireless. My brain could be racing on the trail of a migrating subtropical fly, mysteriously causing a malignant myiasis in Swiss dairy herds, while my body was gently undulating to a languid North African groove.

But today I just hurried in, waved to the owner, and sat myself down on a cushion in front of one of their large Macs. I found the website of Concha Magna, the foremost forensic entomologist in Spain. We'd met once at a conference in London and had since exchanged emails regarding research interests we had in common.

Scrolling through her web pages, I came upon what I was looking for. On La Sirena, at this time of the year, *Calliphora vicinia* would arrive on a body first, before *Sarcophaga canaria*, and become active at 13°C in daylight hours.

This told me that by the time I found Esmeralda, she'd been dead at least ten hours if not more. If she'd been killed on the beach on Saturday evening, the fly I witnessed in the act of ovipositing was most probably the

12

first arrival, as she was cruising alone and it had been just barely warm enough for her to be flying about. A mathematical calculation using the temperatures of the ground, the air, and the body at the time of recovery, would give me a better picture of exactly how long Esmeralda had been dead—if she'd actually died on the beach.

But that was the problem.

There was no way a body could lay in full view on that beach on a Saturday evening, undiscovered all through the night until seven the next morning. She was killed somewhere else, and the killer, or killers, waited until the deserted hours before dawn to arrange the corpse on the sand.

But now we had a witness they hadn't counted on.

There was no way a body could lay in full view on that beach on a Saturday evening, undiscovered, all through the night until seven the next morning. She was killed somewhere else, and the killer, or killers, waited until the deserted hours before dawn to arrange the corpse on the sand. But now we had a witness they hadn't counted on. I thought of that old nursery rhyme: Who Killed Cock Robin?

"Who saw him die? 'I,' said the Fly, with my little eye, I saw him die."

3

The Guardia Civil was most inconveniently located at the summit of a steep hill. It was on the only road that led out of town—or back into town if a car was approaching from the north of the island, or coming from the capital city, San Carlos, on the western coast. Their headquarters were in the grand old style of the Spanish colonists with a roof of terra cotta tiles and second-story wooden balconies cosseting tall, dark green doors that remained shuttered all day long. Flanking the main entrance, the national flag and the Guardia's flag flew side by side.

Our taxi pulled in next to one of the Guardia's off-road vehicles. The driver, not used to delivering tourists to this destination, asked if he should wait for us. Mimmo paid him and sent him back down the hill.

Across the road there was nothing but a steep bank of shrubbery overlooking a dry creek clogged with cacti. In the far distance, I could see the terraced fields and simple stone buildings of a few farmhouses. Next door to the impressive Guardia edifice was an unassuming one-story modern building—the hospital that housed the morgue where Esmeralda's body waited for me.

The reception office was barely big enough for two desks, three plastic chairs and a bookcase. One of the men I'd seen earlier on the beach now occupied one of the chairs, Spanish pop music emanating from his computer. For a moment, this had a relaxing effect on me, until I noticed a poster behind his head entitled *"Las Drogas Abusos,"* with photos and accompanying text arranged in chart form. Without my glasses, I couldn't really read the words, but the green cannabis leaves were at the bottom, and a white powder that might have been heroin or cocaine was in the very first position, with an assortment of tablets and capsules filling in the middle rows of the chart.

Next to this poster, a large football trophy and a statue of the Virgin holding Christ the Little King shared the top shelf of the bookcase.

Clearly, no attempts at separation of Church and State in this country, I thought to myself.

I explained we were there to meet Ballero, and the officer continued eating cashew nuts out of a can while staring at his computer screen. In less than a minute, Ballero poked his head in through the doorway. I rose and introduced Mimmo. In the intervening hours since we'd last seen each other, I'd gathered that Ballero's proper title was "Chief Inspector". It said something favorable about him that during our previous discussion he'd been more interested in my answers to his questions than in his own status. Although I'd repeatedly addressed him only as *"Señor Ballero"*, he had not corrected me.

"Chief Inspector, please allow me to present my husband, Mimmo Massini. He asked to escort me here, and I hope that won't be a problem for you. He could wait somewhere in the hospital, if it's inconvenient to have him in the morgue."

Ballero was affable enough, shook Mimmo's hand and took us out through the back of the Guardia building, into a petite, manicured garden, and then through a locked door at the rear of the hospital. We descended a flight of stairs and entered what appeared to be the morgue, though it didn't resemble anything I'd ever seen in the States, no cameras or high-tech gismos.

I recognized Esmeralda's body lying on a stainless steel table toward the back of the room. She was still on her stomach, but the pathologist from Tenerife, a tall man speaking with an assistant, had already removed the knife. He broke off the conversation and walked over to greet us.

"Dr. Gabriel Nunez," he said, holding out his hand, "You must be the forensic entomologist that the Inspector has been telling me about."

I was instantly relieved by his friendly, informal attitude. He was outfitted in scrubs and a mask, so I couldn't see much of his face, but I did notice a gold stud in his right ear, and from what I could tell from his eyes he seemed a calm and confident man.

I introduced Mimmo and suggested he wait for us in the anteroom. My husband looked across to the autopsy table where Esmeralda's body appeared like a store mannequin, undressed, garishly artificial under the fluorescent lighting. I realized that for him it was an emotional moment. He'd known her much better than I had.

While I'd bonded more with Serenella, her little girl who always wanted to play with Mostly, Mimmo regularly dropped in to the disco late at night and chatted with Esmeralda as she tended bar. Except on weekends, the place was usually quiet around closing time, and they had talked together about business and shared the small town gossip. She had confided a bit about her personal life with him as well. I remembered from my single days, how easy it was to open up to an attractive but safely married man.

"Chief Inspector, you might want to speak more with my husband, as he actually often visited with Esmeralda at her club. Possibly something she might have mentioned to him this past week could help you in some way." Ballero accepted my suggestion with alacrity and proposed the men step outside to smoke.

I could see the relief on both men's faces. Neither actually wanted to witness the autopsy. For my part, as a biologist I'd dissected human and other mammal cadavers enough to feel sufficiently distant from what I was about to experience.

I removed the fly evidence from my backpack, and placed the Styrofoam box containing the fly and her ovary, along with my tools, on the polished stone counter. I also gave Nunez the report I'd written up in Spanish. I explained that I was a research scientist, and that while I was sure that my entomology expertise could help them with the case, I wanted him to understand that I'd never yet acted as an expert police witness, testifying in a trial in the States or in Germany.

In return, he assured me that he was very interested to have the opportunity to work with me, and was most intrigued by what I'd already told Ballero in regards to the time and place of death. He acknowledged that while the body was still cold and stiff with rigor mortis, and that livor mortis—the settling of the blood— was readily apparent, this could only tell him death had occurred somewhere between a half day and 24 hours prior to the time we found her. Without my contribution it would be difficult to ascertain a more precise post-mortem interval. Relying on the victim's stomach contents was a long shot in his opinion, though we could take it into consideration if anything identifiable was found. He also explained that Ballero's preliminary interviews with the victim's family had not turned up any outstanding leads. Knowing exactly when and where she was killed would be very important in leading us to a suspect.

"I requested the police to leave her body face down—until we had a chance to examine it together— because of something I noticed in the hair elastic holding her hair at the back of her head. I was afraid it might get lost or damaged if her head was rotated," I explained.

I put on the scrubs and gloves provided for me and took my forceps over to the autopsy table. Nunez adjusted a large overhead lens to center on the back of her head. Under the strong magnification, what had been barely recognizable to my naked eye when we were on the beach was now fantastically visible. Suspended in a neon pink forest of synthetic fibers, a cream-colored globe hung like a full moon.

I motioned to Nunez to take my place at the lens.

"At first, I thought this was a small petal from a flowering shrub, or tree, but actually it is a floret—a tiny flower itself, from a larger composite flower."

"I see," said Nunez.

In another few seconds, I noticed something else as well.

"Now look very carefully, about three centimeters down from the pink material—at around 4 o'clock from the floret. It's like a brown twig and blends into her hair so well, I didn't notice it before, but strangely enough I believe that is an *insect* leg—from a cricket or a katydid."

Nunez laughed. "Well, I'd have missed that for sure." I was momentarily afraid that maybe he was being facetious.

"Yes, it looks like the spines on the foretibia are hooked into the nylon threads of the hair tie."

I waited for him to say something but he remained at the lens, making minute adjustments. I ventured a theory.

"My guess is that it got there during a struggle—she would have been lying on the ground, her head rolled, perhaps, and the flower and the insect's leg got caught up in the hair tie. There's some other natural debris ... little bits of broken leaves, along with a few grains of sand ... probably from the beach in her hair as well. Do you see that?"

"*Si, si,* you're quite right." "

This, as well as the egg-laying behavior of the *Calliphora* fly, is what originally made me suspect that Esmeralda was not killed on the beach or anywhere *near* her bar."

"But," Nunez paused for a moment to gather his thoughts, "in my experience, a knife wound in the back, at that angle, a single mortal wound, indicates the victim was entirely surprised from behind... and there are no signs of a struggle."

"But the angle? Does it seem as if she were sitting or standing up, or already lying face down?"

"It depends of course to some degree on the height and strength of the perpetrator, but, yes, it does indicate she was already faced down. Of course she may have been sleeping or intoxicated."

"Well, I don't mean to speak badly of the dead, Dr. Nunez, and my acquaintance with Esmeralda was superficial, but I can tell you for certain, she was not a nature lover, not an outdoor person."

I could see by the look on his face that I'd surprised him. I think he'd been expecting I was going to tell him Esmeralda was a drug addict or something.

"Look here at her fingernails." I continued.

The nails were square-tipped, synthetically extended and perfectly lacquered in a frosted shade of lavender. No chips, no tears. They certainly showed no evidence that she'd put up a fight.

"Those are acrylic nails and they cost about 40 Euros a set to get done in a salon. Women who do this are generally not the type to go on long hikes in the woods. She was a businesswoman and something of a workaholic, I would say, and when she wasn't working, she was partying."

"She was a night club owner..."

I jumped in quickly. "You most likely *will* find some amount of alcohol or drugs in her blood tests, but she *never* would have been out in some natural spot on the island, voluntarily lying on the ground, rolling her head on the forest floor. If we can get a botanist to identify that flower, and I get a better look under the scope at the cricket leg, we may even manage to target the exact location where she was killed."

Nunez seemed intrigued and agreeable. He cut the hair tie loose with a sharp pair of scissors, and I worked carefully to remove the flower and the leg from the tangle of threads and hair. Together we slowly scavenged her tresses for any other minute detritus that could be still clinging to her thick curls. We kept talking as we worked.

"But why, Dr. Jerome, does a petal and a cricket's leg mean to you a wild spot on the island? Why not in her garden or someone else's garden?"

"Please, call me Epiphany," I asked. "Well, botany is not my specialty, though as you know, there is a strong co-evolutionary relationship between insects and plants, so most entomologists are interested in and have some knowledge of botany."

Nunez nodded. I felt encouraged to proceed.

"While I've been here I've tried to learn as much as I can about the endemic insects *and* plants. Given the extraordinary geology and location of this island, it's not surprising there are many plants and insects known only to here or one or two of the other Canary Islands. This leg, I'm pretty sure, belongs to the family Tettigoniidae, making it what we commonly call a 'katydid' in English, or *'grillo'* in Spanish."

I took the leg over to where I'd set up my scope and switched on the light. It took me a moment to find the right level of magnification and depth of focus to confirm my initial assessment. I stepped aside so that Nunez could get a look as well.

"Katydids mate like crickets do, using an acoustical system. They do their calling with a stridulation instrument on their forewings, but their 'ears' are on their legs. Here, can you see that dark rough area near the 'knee'?"

Nunez made a sound of assent.

"In katydids the system is a little more specialized. They have a membrane that runs down the leg connecting the tympanal organ to a spiracle on their thorax, which of course we can't see here, because we *only* have the leg. But we are able to see a dark split or line in the cuticle of the femor which indicates the *presence* of that inner membrane—the acoustical trachea."

Nunez mumbled, "Mmm hmm."

"I can't believe how lucky we are! The one leg that got tangled in her hair was the foreleg, or else I could have never known for sure that this was a Tettigoniidae because that specialization is *only* found on the forelegs, not on any of their other legs. And without the rest of the *grillo* I wouldn't know who the hell we had here!"

Nunez looked up from the scope, pulled down his mask and I could see he was laughing at me. He was a very handsome man with a wonderful smile. I found myself wondering if he was married.

He reached for a bottle of water from a pack standing on a nearby counter. Then he politely pulled out another one and handed it over to me.

"Claro. I believe you that this is a *grillo*, but what does this tell us about the location of the killing, and about the flower?"

I felt myself blushing. I realized I was getting way ahead of myself, and I wasn't used to proceeding with the deliberate, careful pace of a forensic pathologist looking at a criminal case.

I took a moment to gulp down some water. "Okay. I'm getting a little ahead of the game here, I grant you that. But this is where I'd like to take it, although we *do* need a botanist, preferably Juan Lopez from the *Parque*, as he's the most knowledgeable person on the ecology of the microhabitats of the island."

Nunez, I could see, was really interested in what I was saying, so I continued, trying to be clear but concise. We both wanted to get to the knife wound, and he had a lot more work to do on her autopsy.

"Katydids use vegetation for their inactive periods, mainly for camouflage and protection, so they are normally associated with a very specific type of vegetation. In some species, their wings have evolved to resemble the leaves of their habitat."

"And you think this cricket is related in some way to this flower?"

"I suspect there are maybe only two, at the most three species here on the island, and they're likely to be found at the higher elevations where there's more moisture and more trees. The blossom, when identified, might give us a picture of the microhabitat where it grows. If we're lucky, the vegetation that this *grillo* hangs out in, and the plant that produced this flower, may only occur *together* in a very limited territory."

"Like where hypothetically?" he asked.

"Like on the western slope of the cloud belt which is 700 to 900 meters up the mountain. That's an example of a region which dictates very restricted conditions, very particular humidity and light conditions."

For a pathologist, Nunez certainly had a cheerful manner that inspired collaboration. I carried on.

"But this island is full of unique conditions; that's *why* there is such a diversity of life here and..."

"Yes," he interrupted. "But the roads through the mountains are slow driving. I know, I've been here before on vacation. If you can calculate from the eggs the maximum and minimum interval between the time of death and when you discover the body, it should be possible to eliminate a good portion of the island through distances alone."

"When did Ballero say Esmeralda was last seen alive?" I asked. "That of course would be our maximum time, if she'd been killed right here in town almost immediately afterwards."

"Around 11:00 Saturday morning. And you found her at 7:00 this morning..."

"So say that our maximum possibility is..." I was taking a moment to do the simple math in my head, never a shining moment for me.

Nunez got there quicker. "We're working within 20 hours. So if you can get an ecological parameter of where it *could* have happened, then yes, considering the travel times around the island, you could get even closer to the murder scene, and narrow the post-mortem interval, but those are a lot of *ifs*!"

I wanted to qualify what I was suggesting. "Flies and beetles are my field, not crickets and grasshoppers, but we can consult an Orthopteran specialist at the National Museum in Madrid, someone who's probably collected here on the island and knows more about each species' associations. Put that together with what Dr. Lopez can tell us about this flower blossom, and we might be able to get a pretty confined vicinity, and at the very least, rule out her garden or the cultivated areas around town that Esmeralda..."

Nunez finished my sentence for me, "... *normally* frequented."

"Exactly!" I was happy he was following my train of thought so well. "And that should send Ballero looking for *who* or *what* could have lured her so completely out of the range of her regular patterns of movement."

Nunez's assistant was also from Tenerife, a technician from his own lab. By the time we got to the wound, he'd completed his work on the knife.

There were no fingerprints to be found. I wasn't surprised.

The killer didn't need a tide table. He knew where to dump the body before high tide. Any tracks would be gone by the time she was discovered after daylight, when the tide had receded. It wasn't likely they would forget to wear gloves, or wipe the knife clean, but why leave it behind at all?

"It's not easy to pull out a long thin curved blade that's penetrated this deep," Nunez explained to me, "The swifter the movement, the easier it is to push it straight through, especially with a sharp tip, but it takes quite a lot of strength and time to pull it back out."

Before we'd examined the material from Esmeralda's hair, the technician had removed her clothes, putting them carefully into paper bags and sealing them with official tape. Nunez took notes, commenting into a handheld recorder, first on the natural evidence extracted from her hair, and then on the size, location and appearance of the fatal knife wound. The assistant took photographs.

The wound—a one-inch slit—slightly gaped and terminated at each end in points. This indicated that the blade was double-edged, something we already knew.

An irregular bruising on the skin near the wound caused by the force of the knife's hilt confirmed Nunez's opinion on the trajectory of the blade.

"Look," he said, "the blade slipped through the protection of the rib cage, penetrating at an angle into the left ventricle of the heart, causing rapid fatal bleeding into the pericardial cavity and the lungs."

Now it was my turn.

Nunez adjusted the overhead light so that I could see into the wound with the aid of a magnifying lens clipped to my glasses.

There was a strong chance that any eggs left behind by my fly had been destroyed by the removal of the weapon. Normally, a forensic entomologist is given the opportunity to search the body before the pathologist begins the autopsy, but in these unconventional circumstances, I had luck on my side.

As I swabbed delicately beneath the beveled, lower edge of the wound, at the shallow depth where I expected to find a possible clutch of eggs, the fine bristles of my sable paintbrush revealed them like a dainty pearl poised on the edge of an open clam. They stuck easily to the brush as I deftly transferred them to a slide.

"Voilà!" I cried, quite pleased with myself.

I checked carefully for other traces of infestation of the wound, and after a minute or two found more eggs tucked between the thick layer of connective tissues below the epidermis, where many broken capillaries provided the ideal environment for fly larvae to flourish. I extracted them and stored them in a separate vial, as it was still possible that another fly had deposited eggs earlier, or even later than Madam Fly's brood.

"I confess, I'm surprised that there's so little infestation," I told Nunez. "But that in itself might be telling us something. Medications or drugs in the blood can repel flies from laying their eggs. Or maybe this fly I caught was just the early bird arrival."

"Well, we should get a preliminary toxicology report pretty quickly," said Nunez.

"We need to get fresh eggs to Madrid as quickly as possible, to Concha Magna's lab," I instructed him.

"It used to be the only way we had for determining species from eggs and early instar larvae—I'm sorry, that's what we say for *maggots*, instar is the stages of development before they become adult flies. It used to be the only way was to raise them out on liver in a temperature-controlled situation that mimicked field conditions. Believe me, no one wanted you in their lab; the stink was so horrific!"

Nunez laughed. "I can imagine."

"But now we have a technique using gel electrophoresis and analysis of the flies' allozyme markers." I took a deep breath; I didn't want to sound too eager.

"It's very fast; we can do it in about three hours. It's cheaper and more accurate than conventional DNA work using mitochondrial gene expression. But since it depends on a comparative procedure, you must have a continual availability of control samples from all regional species. I'm pretty hopeful that Concha will have the Canary Islands covered in her library of samples, but I'll call her and ask. Do you think we can get the eggs to her quickly?"

Nunez nodded. "I return on the boat at 18:30. I can send them to the airport with someone from our lab in Tenerife as soon as I get back. If you give me the telephone number we'll alert her as to when she can expect them in Madrid."

Together we examined the anal opening before turning Esmeralda over on to her back. I knew with such minimal infestation of the more attractive stab wound that it was unlikely I'd find anything in the body's natural openings. One of the first rules of good forensic work is that you don't rule out any possibilities until all the physical evidence has been gathered; you let your findings construct the hypothesis, not the other way around.

When I touched her, I was surprised at how cold she felt through the sheer latex of my gloves. I'd told Ballero that when I found her I checked her pulse but she was already cold. In the coolness of the morgue, she seemed even colder and void of any presence at all. Her face was discolored with the dark mottling of livor mortis. I thought about the last time I'd seen her, very early Friday morning at the fish truck.

Every Friday, as soon as it was light, the truck came up from the docks, raucous Spanish horn music blaring through the loudspeaker on the roof of the cab, urging housewives to buy fresh fish for the weekend. It stopped on the street below our bedroom window. That morning, I threw on a pair of shorts and a shirt and went out to get some octopus.

Esmeralda had already finished with her shopping when I reached the truck. A trendy purse was slung over her shoulder; her arms were full of fish wrapped in plastic bags. We exchanged greetings but didn't linger to talk. Even at that early hour, she already had a hurried air about her.

I could find no trace of what I remembered of her now in the vacant face, the eyes open without seeing. Grains of dark sand clung to her lashes, the fine creases in her face, her lips, and the fine hairs inside her nose. Her features were like a lunar landscape: hills, valleys, and craters that signified nothing but territory to be explored.

Fernel, a famous sixteenth-century French doctor, while trying to understand the physiology of death, once wrote in his journal: "We recognize our friend although his life is no longer there. The innate heat has fled."

But for me, so much more than heat flees.

4

Ballero was alone and shouting at me from the top of the hospital stairs. "Your husband said you should take a taxi and meet him at Fellini's when you're done here at the morgue." I was curious if he'd learned anything helpful from Mimmo, but at the moment we had something more important to discuss. I took him back with me into the lab, and showed him the material from Esmeralda's hair hoping he'd understand its significance in finding the crime scene. Talking with Ballero was much different than working with Nunez, a man trained in science.

Ballero was many years older than Nunez, and a big man on a little island. Literally, Ballero was big—tall and wide in girth—but considering the power he and his family held locally, he dominated more than the physical space he occupied. Looking into Ballero's hazel brown eyes, opaque pools beneath bushy grey eyebrows, there was something there that I could not fathom.

He turned toward Nunez as if deferring to the younger man and his far greater experience with murder investigations.

"I think she's quite right. This didn't happen on the beach." Nunez pointed to Esmeralda's feet. "No shoes recovered, and no sand on the soles of her feet or between the toes. It does make me believe the body was dumped there."

He showed Ballero the perfectly manicured hands.

"Not even a torn fingernail—there's no sign that she struggled. From what you and Epiphany have said, I think using the hair evidence to reconstruct her movements before the murder is your best chance so far. Or do you have something better from your interviews with the victim's family and friends?"

Ballero wagged his round balding head from side to side, indicating a negative.

"We found her car parked on the Punta, but there was nothing significant inside. No one seems to know where she was on Saturday afternoon or evening. Her bartender said she'd told him she would be late, but when she didn't show up at all at the club, he was too busy on his own to worry about it. He tried her mobile once, but it was turned off. Her daughter was the last one to see her around 11:00 on Saturday morning," replied Ballero, and his voice softened with this last remark.

Breaking an awkward silence, Ballero offered that since it was Sunday, it could be difficult to get hold of Dr. Lopez, but he promised he would put one of his men on it.

I told him to ring me on Mimmo's phone as soon as they reached the botanist, and I would bring the blossom to Lopez if he wanted to meet somewhere other than Ballero's headquarters.

Nunez and I agreed to confer before the boat for Tenerife departed later in the early evening. I suggested the only bar on the docks, the one Mimmo always referred to as the "Once a Day." He always said that if you sat there all day, it was possible to find anyone you were looking for, as everyone in town migrated through at least once a day.

I packed up my things and called a taxi to take me back down to the harbor, to Fellini's where Mimmo would no doubt be drinking. I hoped he'd remembered to stop by Udo's to pick up Mostly.

When I stepped out of the hospital and back into the afternoon sun, the heat was staggering, and yet I felt like the chill of the morgue room would never leave my bones. Now that I was no longer under Nunez and Ballero's scrutiny, my professional distance and demeanor had worn off. I felt depressed and shaken by the experience of examining Esmeralda's body. I thought about Amy and how she regularly worked on human corpses in far worse condition than Esmeralda, though I was sure she'd never had to work on someone that she'd known, as I just had.

Looking at my watch, I mentally turned back the clock eight hours to California time. Could I wake Amy up at 7:00 am on a Sunday morning?

No, I'd have to wait until at least noon, which meant I might as well call her after I talked again with Nunez, and that way I might have more to tell her then, anyway, but maybe not.

I tried to enjoy the ride back down the mountain, the beautiful view of the ocean, sparkling under a cloudless sky. But instead I felt deflated, hungry, and nervous, as well as unsure of my intentions. Was I getting blindly involved in a local crime I didn't really understand? Would Ballero tell Constanze Therese that I was helping the investigation? I couldn't imagine explaining to her that I'd poked into her daughter's eyes, ears, nose and mouth, let alone her vaginal and anal cavities, for traces of fly infestation. Ballero *had* asked me not to discuss the case with anyone, and I assured him that of course I wouldn't. I just hoped to God he had the sense not to tell anyone I was working with him. He probably wouldn't. What would it gain him? It would only be showing his hand, and though he seemed, well, *provincial*, he wasn't a stupid man—not in the least.

Fellini's was the Italian hangout in town, a cozy pizzeria squeezed into two rooms on a viewless back alley close to the docks. Peppe and his twin sister Lola, Fellini's owners, had learned pizza making from their grandfather in Naples. Peppe really looked the part, a younger, only slightly thinner Pavarotti, all in white: T- shirt, long apron and traditional cap. He commanded over a compact, open kitchen, while Lola, in beaded dreadlocks and low-cut tank tops that showed off her tattoos, worked the bar and served tables in the back room where customers watched movies in Italian on a widescreen TV.

The twins and twelve or so other local characters, plus the occasional seasonal tourists, made up an improvised but tight-knit Italian community, found almost any evening in its entirety at Fellini's. It was rather like an adaptation of the timeless *passeggiata*—the ritual early evening parade in the heart of most small towns in Italy—the aimless strolling around with one's family and friends before retiring to the privacy of home. As Mimmo calls it in English, 'Birds of a feather flock together'. But I tried as a zoologist to explain to him this is not strictly true. Only gregarious birds consistently keep the company of their own kind. It's true though. If Italians were birds, they'd be a gregarious breed like parakeets or crows.

Sunday was a popular movie night as there was no cinema in the town and most people were recovering from the drinking and dancing of Friday and Saturday nights. As Peppe had just opened for the afternoon, I found Mimmo alone with him, helping to clean mushrooms, fastidiously wiping each one with a damp paper towel, before placing it on a wooden cutting board for Peppe to slice. Mimmo was drinking Ramazotti and Mostly appeared to be fast asleep in his lap, despite the loud reggae music playing from the sound system. Mimmo smiled happily as I entered.

"Hallo, Meez Marple!" He hailed me. I glared back. Fortunately, it seemed Peppe didn't include old Margaret Rutherford movies in his film collection.

I greeted Peppe and asked for a Ramazotti as well. I could tell from his somber face that he and my husband had been discussing Esmeralda's murder. I was sure that by now there was no other topic of conversation anywhere in town. Surely, Mimmo would have sense enough not to leak the extent of my involvement, other than that I had found her body, which everyone would eventually find out anyway. I looked into my husband's *Ramazottied* smile to assess whether any damage control was needed.

"I guess Mimmo told you that I discovered Esmeralda's body early this morning on the beach?" I asked in Spanish, as Peppe spoke no English and I couldn't call on my shaky Italian after such a long, hard day.

Peppe rolled his big round eyes, and did that typical Italian shoulder shrug with palms together gesture that means so many words that can't be said. Then, motioning for me to finish my glass, he poured me another round of the bitters. I slumped on the stool and thought about slyly prying some information out from 'Italian Central,' as I had nicknamed the bar. His sister was a different story. Even though Lola was there almost as much as her brother, she remained somewhat aloof from the clientele of Fellini's and was not inclined to gossip.

"Ever have a murder here before?" I asked.

"Long time ago," Peppe waved to the past with his hand like he was throwing salt over his shoulder. "Some guy in Hermosa hit his brother, when they were drunk and fighting—so hard he killed him—but that was before we came here."

"What's the local law enforcement like?

"Corrupt," said Peppe simply.

"In what way?" I glanced nervously over at Mimmo. *Don't you dare open your mouth,* my eyes said.

"They don't do shit except make sure the rich get richer."

"Well, what I mean is, are they likely to find Esmeralda's murderer and get the right person?"

"Depends on who did it," said Peppe, "and why they did it."

That was exactly what I didn't want to hear. I was also afraid that if Mimmo believed Peppe's cynical viewpoint, he would insist I quit 'playing detective' immediately, and drag me back to Berlin.

"Was Esmeralda liked by people?" I asked trying another tactic.

"She was respected, *basta*."

"Esmeralda was a good woman," Mimmo, who has a generous nature and a large yardstick by which he measures others, went to her defense.

Peppe had another perspective.

"Look, everyone knows she was a good mama to the little girl, and that after the papa drowned when the kid was just a baby, she became very depressed. But slowly, slowly, all she cared about was making money. Some people tried to stop her from opening that club, but she outsmarted them and that made her a lot of enemies. In this place there's not so much money to go around. The ferry can only bring so many people here each day, and now the way the economies are going... every day there is less and less to go around."

"But then why are they rebuilding the harbor to accommodate large cruise ships?" I asked.

"They were forced to do that. The *Canarias* government got money from the EU expressly for that purpose, to promote development, but meanwhile most of the businesses here are suffering as the tourists aren't coming because of all the noise and dirt ... two years now it's been like this."

"But there is so much construction going on all around here," said Mimmo, "not just at the harbor."

"And who owns those buildings?" demanded Peppe. "Germans and international corporations, not local people."

"Yeah, but local people sold them the land," I put in.

"Exactly," answered Peppe. "Rich people like Esmeralda's mother and

31

Hector Ballero..."

By now, the second Ramazotti on an empty stomach was taking a toll. I didn't want to wait for the time it would take for a pizza, so I asked Peppe for a plate of antipasti. While he sliced the cheeses and meats, I considered the information he'd just given me.

"So what you're telling me is that local people have no say over what's happening to their island, because the wealthiest landowners have sold off most of the properties to international interests for tourist development?"

Peppe looked at me in disbelief. "This is a surprise to you, Epiphany, that Spain has become Germany's banana republic?"

Mimmo snorted and then said something in Italian that I didn't get. Both men laughed. Then I realized it was "killing the chicken that lays the golden egg."

I said, "Goose, it's supposed to be goose, not a chicken."

"In Italian it's a chicken," insisted Mimmo.

At that moment Mimmo's phone rang. He pulled it out of his shirt pocket and checked the caller ID, then handed it over to me. I heard Ballero's gravelly voice on the other end. He told me they'd finally located Lopez, and the scientist was going to be having dinner with friends at seven o'clock at the Mirador, and that he'd readily agreed to help us with the case.

I looked at my watch, I had plenty of time to call Amy before I had to meet with Nunez at the bar on the docks, but it would be earlier than I'd originally intended. Too bad, Amy would just have to wake up and talk.

Then, when the pathologist left on the ferry at six thirty, I could get a taxi to take me up to the Mirador, a restaurant designed by the famous Spanish architect, Cesar Manrique. Constructed entirely from the native volcanic rock, it perched on the edge of a steep canyon with a spectacular view of the whole valley and the ocean horizon. The sun would just be setting around the time of our meeting, but after this last conversation about local politics, I was growing more apprehensive, and not in the mood for beauty.

5

In the 15th century, when European sailors first came to La Sirena they called it 'the Lost Island'. At certain times of the year, due to its particular geographical position, when the high trade winds from the Atlantic meet the lower, warmer winds coming off the Saharan desert, clouds and thick fog stagnate on the mountain peaks, then slowly drop down like a theater curtain to sea level, causing the entire island to literally disappear from sight.

On most days, when approaching La Sirena by boat, it appears in the distance like the hump of a camel rising up out of the water. Formed by the accretion of volcanic matter cast up through fissures in the ocean floor, the island formed when the African continent halted its movement some five million years ago, in the Tertiary period. Heavy erosion from precipitation carved out deep ravines in the interior of the camel's hump—what Spanish settlers called *barrancos*—while the sea sculpted the steep exterior basalt walls that span from the highest altitudes down to the coast.

How the island eventually came to be named 'the mermaid' by Spaniards has been lost among its other legends. Historians believe that the original inhabitants of La Sirena were a Berber tribe that made their way from Africa in small boats.

When the dry winds blow from the Sahara, they carry very fine particles of sand in suspension, and no matter how hard you try to keep it out, this dust is everywhere—an invisible coating on the cellophane of new CDs, on computer keys, or between your teeth.

Despite all the dust, soil is still the most scant resource on Sirena. Ecologically, you can divide the island into three zones where very different climates give rise to distinct ecosystems.

At the coastline and below 700 meters, the habitat is dry, subtropical. Neatly irrigated banana plantations and exotic cacti compete for space with native succulents and euphorbias, seen nowhere else in the world. Early farmers learned to terrace the ravines, building retaining walls from the volcanic rock they cleared from the soil.

Above the dry zone, rising up to 1000 meters, is the transition zone, which gets most of the winter rains. Lastly, the top 500 meters is the wet zone, where the temperatures never exceed 18°C, and thick fogs cling to relict forests of laurel trees, remnant species of Lauraceae, which once covered the whole Mediterranean region 10,000 years ago, before the basin became warmer and drier during the end of the Pleistocene.

These primeval forests are the lungs of the island. Water from the clouds distills on the broad surface of the laurel leaves and then drips down into the earth, from which it eventually seeps back up as life-giving springs. A small brown beetle, rarely sighted and found only in association with these laurel trees, was my reason for choosing La Sirena for our holiday in the sun.

A colleague of mine at the museum in Berlin asked me, when he heard I was planning to vacation in the Canaries, if I might consider going to La Sirena to find some female *Broscus crassimargo* for DNA samples for his research. He was working on evolutionary trends in the family Carabidae and how volcanic events may have directed speciation in this part of the world. Mimmo had been here once before when he was younger, and he readily agreed that we might enjoy it more than some of the larger islands better developed for tourism.

A "working holiday" is how Mimmo referred to our trip because I spent so much time hiking and looking for insects, while his idea of a good time is thermoregulating his body like a lizard in the sun, or drinking and chatting in the bars and cafes. I guess you could say that when we travel together we each seek out our own natural habitats.

On arrival, our very first stop after disembarking from the ferry was Café Sport. Udo was tending the bar and there was only one customer, a construction worker nursing a beer. My husband is incurably social. After only one glass of Chianti and some *tapas*, he had Udo, who fits the despondent Germanic stereotype, laughing and telling stories about famous musicians who travel to the island to record with some English producer who built a studio here. Meanwhile, I pumped the Spanish builder about places to rent, and he told me about Constanze Therese, who lived just up the road and owned the new apartments adjacent to Café Sport.

Udo explained that the harbor was being expanded and deepened so large cruise ships could dock in the future, bringing in more tourists, the kind you typically find on the larger islands.

We arrived on a Sunday, so it was quiet, but we could see empty cranes and bulldozers parked near the dockyard. Udo complained that most of the tourists had resorted to staying further up the coast because the construction dirt and the noise had been just too much. The development work was killing his business. We later found out this new construction was going on all over the sunnier, leeward side of the island. It was not the place Mimmo remembered.

Udo told us that Constanze Therese was also his landlord, and that she hadn't mentioned the construction plans at the time he renewed his lease. She claimed she hadn't known either, and that now as a result she couldn't rent out her fancy new apartments for forty Euros a day. Udo thought the apartments had been empty recently and we could get one for half that amount. I was tired from traveling and suggested we take an apartment and try it out. If the noise was that bad, we could go looking again when we were rested up. We were staying a month, so there was time enough to find something more suitable. There was only one large expensive hotel in the little harbor town, so this seemed a better temporary arrangement.

The land surrounding Constanze Therese's *casa* was a triumph of man over nature. It seemed as though her house had been dropped onto a patchwork quilt of tidy geometric agricultural gardens, nestled between rocky coast and the shelter of the cliffs. Like ancient stone gods, the looming presence of the cliffs gave the structures below a toy-like appearance.

We climbed up broad steps lined with over-sized ceramic containers of flaming scarlet *coleus* plants. Pale green beads of Donkey's Tails spilled over the rims of the pots, while pink-tipped fingers of *crassulacea* crept along the ground beneath them. We ascended above the crowns of fragrant orange trees and passed a wire aviary where a pair of bright green parrots, absorbed in grooming their feathers, ignored us.

Two middle-aged men sat on the ocean-facing terrace, playing dominos and smoking cigars. I thought one might possibly be Constanze Therese's husband, but later I was to learn that hers was a family of women only. Any men sighted on her property were laboring for her in some form or another.

"Buenas tardes," Mimmo greeted them in his Italian-accented Spanish,

"buscamos Constanze Therese."

The men barely looked up from their game, but one nodded his head in the direction of an open-air kitchen. We crossed the large terrace and peered into the kitchen, calling *"Hola?"*

Beyond the kitchen, a woman sat watching television in a cozy sitting room. She motioned to us to enter into the house and signaled again for us to sit on a sofa piled with fussy, crochet-covered pillows. We obeyed. Above us, a wall-ensconced, gold-leafed Madonna, with modest eyes half-closed gazed down upon us.

A cat strolled in from the terrace where it had previously been curled up on a basket of laundry, and looked up suspiciously at Mostly in my arms, then let out one strangled, prolonged complaint, turned with its tail raised defiantly, and left the room. Mostly quivered in repressed exasperation but remained on my lap.

Of course, Constanze Therese knew we were just another couple of strangers looking for a place to stay, but she engaged us in polite conversation as if pleasantries should always come before business. In retrospect, I understood that this relaxed friendliness was a way to gauge our financial status, to ascertain the maximum rate that could be extracted from us.

When she understood that Mimmo was Italian, her face lit up. I realized that once she'd been very pretty, but now her body sagged with resignation, and when not occupied in momentary flirtation, her facial features were like well-worn fixtures on a closed door.

"I love Italians," she said looking at me with renewed interest.

"Well, actually, I'm not Italian, I come from California. I'm Mexican-American."

Her expression downshifted.

"But we met in Italy," I went on somewhat apologetically, "we met at the wedding of an Italian friend from Berlin, where we live now."

I began to become, as I sometimes do, overwhelmed by my own story as I try to explain it to a person who has never even been very far from where they were born. I was raised in two languages in two cultures, and through my work I came to live in another country whose language I must learn. But I am also married to a man from yet another country, and because his language is close enough to my own I can naturally speak a little in his language, while he can speak even more of my language. Although generally we conduct most of our relationship in English, it is really a second language for me, and a fourth for him.

Then, of course, she and I acknowledged that the Spanish I spoke was quite different to Sirenian Spanish, which was also clearly different from what is known as *Castellano*, spoken on most of the mainland of Spain. We had to work at comprehending each other as some words and pronunciations were so dissimilar. When all this was finally out of the way, we got down to the business at hand of actually seeing one of her apartments.

She reached over to the center of the coffee table to a green glass ashtray to fish out one key from a tangle of many.

"Serenella, *ven aqui.*"

A little girl appeared in the doorway. She was at that interesting age when a girl is still a child but her body is changing subtly, anticipating the young woman she will someday be. Wearing shorts, her bare legs seemed more than half of her entire height. Straight, light brown hair was held away from her face with a pink cotton headband. That face, dominated by big grey eyes fringed with long dark lashes, was oddly serene for all her childish energy. She laughed at the sight of Mostly, and knelt down near the couch so that she could pet him.

"Hello," I said, "my name's Epiphany and this is Mostly."

"That's a funny name."

"Which name, Mostly or Epiphany?"

"Mostly," she said the unfamiliar English word hesitantly.

"It means *principalmente* in *Inglés*." I explained.

"And your name, what does it mean?"

"The Epiphany was the day that the Three Kings arrived to bring the presents to the Baby Jesus."

"Oh, yes." The little girl nodded in recognition of the story.

"And I was born on that day, January 6th, so that is what my mother wanted to call me. What is your name again?"

"Serenella, it's an Italian name, my grandmother likes Italian things."

"Ah, *Serenella*," Mimmo chimed in, "The little calm one, you must have been a good baby!" By now, Mostly had jumped from my lap and was standing on his hind legs trying to kiss Serenella. "Go on," instructed Constanze Therese, "take them down to number five." She entrusted the key to the little girl.

"It rents for 25 Euros a day, 20 if you stay the whole month," she said in our direction. "We give you clean linen once a week, and you just let us know if there is something you need, but the kitchen is well equipped."

"Does it have an Italian espresso pot?" asked Mimmo laughing, "That's the only true necessity."

Constanze Therese nodded vigorously and waved her gold-ringed fingers, "*No problemo*, we find you one."

In the weeks that followed we saw more of Serenella than her grandmother for it was always she that brought things down to us: the weekly linen, a lamp for reading, an extra cushion for a chair. We saw her almost daily in the hot afternoons, when she came to find Mostly to play with him in the shallow waters below the tide line. She threw his tennis ball farther and farther into the gentle wave action, and Mostly delighted her with his stubborn, fearless swimming to recover the ball and bring it back.

We gradually became inured to the noise of the building work that only stopped for three hours in the late afternoon during siesta. When it resumed again in the early evening we were gone, walking on the trails away from the town. After that first night, it never occurred to us to look for other rooms in another part of town. I had become enchanted by the towering stone cliffs, and I loved to sit on our balcony and watch them almost indiscernibly shifting color and form as if they were somehow alive. But of course, this illusion was only a trick of the changing light reflecting off the placid water as the sun and the moon made their appointed rounds.

When I now remember the peace I felt in those early days of our vacation, I also think of a cautionary remark I once read in an insightful travel book—that in most holiday places where the water is calm, the people are angry.

6

I dialed in the code from my phone card at the open-air pay phone with the great view overlooking the sea, the one in front of the Moroccan restaurant, Habibe.

My 6 Euro balance would buy me more than an hour's worth of time talking with Amy, but I didn't have that much time before my date with Nunez. A woman's voice, singing desolately in Arabic, drifted out from the open doors of the restaurant. A wind was picking up off the ocean. The terrace was empty, with the few sunset watchers sitting inside. That was good for me. I didn't want anyone overhearing my conversation, though the likelihood of people understanding my rapid English was slim.

In front of me, the great Atlantic Ocean stretched far beyond my horizon. Half a world away, in her apartment in a little Vietnamese neighborhood in San Jose—which she lovingly referred to as "Ho Chi Minh Jose"— Amy picked up the telephone next to her bed.

"Gardiner here," she mumbled, sounding half unconscious.

"Audrey Hepburn?" I asked.

"Is that you, Sophia Loren?" Her voice was quickly coming to life and normal volume.

"Sorry for waking you but I need you, and..."

"No problemo sweetie, wassup? You calling from Berlin? Jeez, you sound like you're right next door..."

"I'm on a little island in the Canaries off the coast of Western Sahara."

"Nice to have a rich husband! Well, nice to have a husband at all..."

"I have a dead body," I said.

"No kidding! Well, I'll trade mine for yours sight unseen. I'm on a horrible, horrible trial right now. Have you heard about the Danny Chesterfield case over there?"

I was about to say, "No, I can barely keep up with the real news," when she added, "No, that's stupid. It's just really a big deal here."

"Go on," I said.

"The defendant is a real creepo. He kidnapped and killed this beautiful little eight year-old girl while her family was camping in Arroyo Seco, but the body was only found six weeks later. They called me in to the recovery scene, and it was a mess, as you can imagine. The coyotes had got at parts of her and the torso was mostly mummified—with the dermestid beetles chewing like mad on it, right? But the head wasn't in the same condition— as though it had somehow been covered and not exposed as long as the torso—but the recovery team never found any evidence for that. Anyway, there were *several* unusual aspects, but I set the PMI earlier than the expert witness that the defense brought in. You know who it was?"

I didn't have a second to respond.

"Get this—*Mason Denby*, that arrogant prick from Tennessee y'know, and he disagreed with me! I mean what the fuck does *he* know about California chaparral fauna after a long drought spell? Well, the point is Chesterfield had a tight alibi around the time the death would have had to have taken place under the PMI Denby proposed, which was around *five* weeks, so it really rocks the prosecution's case, and there's not ... Oh shit I'm sorry, you don't need to hear all this, I guess I'm just still really wound up over it. Denby just took the stand on Friday."

"It's okay," I tried to interject.

"Yeah, I always think I'm going to get to some like *Buddhist* plane or something, where I don't get all worked up about how crazy and unfair this world is, but I don't, or if I do, I sure can't stay there long no matter how hard I try."

"You mean after all those Kung Fu movies you watch and kickboxing classes you take, you're still an emotional *woman*?" I teased her.

She started laughing, "Hey Sophia, I really miss you. Why'd you have to go all Eurotrash on me?" she whined.

"Because I had to get the hell out of San Jose! Now, listen to me, Audrey, and go make coffee while I tell you about this weird thing that's happening to me."

I could hear Amy banging around in her kitchen while I told her my story. She listened patiently with just one-word exclamations here and there until I began to describe the sexy, laid-back Nunez.

"Damn, and you already have a great husband! You should see the Medical Examiners I get to work with."

Finally, when I was done, she had three words of advice. "You go girl!"

I laughed. "What do you mean, go back to Berlin?"

"No, you get on this case. Why not? You've just been in that dusty East Berlin museum too long. Here's your chance to have some real fun. I mean, Christ, that homeboy Ballero sounds completely worthless, and Antonio Banderas is going back to the big city where he's got way more things on his mind, and basically his job is over once he organizes his report. From what you tell me about the Guardia Civil, they're just imported flunkies who aren't supposed to fraternize with the locals. Who the hell has the smarts and the will to put all the pieces together to see justice is done?"

"Me," I said, smiling at the way Amy always made me feel like a heroine in a movie.

This had started years ago, on a stormy Sunday, when it was raining so hard we couldn't go out to do our fieldwork; neither of us had a boyfriend or even the prospect of a date. As Amy so aptly put it, "Let's face it. We've got nothing to look forward to but a thousand stinking flies, and an advisor breathing down our necks who's even a bigger stinker than all them flies!"

That afternoon we baked and ate chocolate chip cookies, then watched old movies on TMC: *Charade* with Audrey Hepburn and Carey Grant, and then Sophia Loren in *Two Women*. Amy said we'd once been those two glamorous movie stars in the 1960's—the physical resemblances were so remarkable—but we'd been reincarnated as entomology grad students to punish us for our vanity. It became our running joke, and in some mysterious way improved my self-esteem. Then we began embellishing it

43

further by making the people who were around us, like our advisor, movie stars as well. He became the insidious Peter Lorre, a little man with a round head and pop eyes, soft-spoken but seething with menace.

"Look, Sophia, you got a weather station on that island somewhere near that beach?" Now Amy was all business. "Yeah, there's this German trekking place here and they run a private one," I replied. "So you'll have accurate data for the hours between when she was last seen and your recovery, right?"

"I'm not too worried about the calculations, I just have to get lucky on that katydid leg and the blossom. Otherwise, unless Ballero has come up with some great clues and he's playing poker with me, there's nothing to go on. Nunez and I felt the body was probably wrapped in a plastic tarp while being transported, because it was so clean—nothing off her clothes like a blanket fiber or anything, well at least that we could find ourselves." I hastily explained to Amy the extreme topography of the island, andthen speculated, "If her body was at a higher, colder elevation wrapped in a tarp or in the trunk of a car for several hours before they brought it down to the beach, then that would have slowed down the decomposition."

"First, talk to that botanist guy. If you can target the location of the murder, you can calculate the possible temp discrepancies and even more importantly, I think you'll get some insight into why she went to that area of the island, and then you'll get closer to the M.O. Sounds like the girl might have had more than enough enemies, but the thing that sticks out like a pink elephant is, why go to all the trouble of bringing her down to that beach where naturally she'd get found right away? Why not leave her hidden in the mountains somewhere?"

"That's been bothering me as well. Her club was on the beach and her home was nearby. You know, it's like they were flaunting the murder."

"It's *something* emotional," Amy said, "but premeditated."

"That's what I was thinking, like they wanted her to be found for some reason."

"Maybe they thought it would seem like someone, a lover maybe, had killed her like in an argument sitting on the beach. They'd have no way of knowing otherwise, of knowing that it could be possible to find out so much from environmental evidence."

"That's possible. Although Nunez told me it's difficult to pull out a knife from that deep in the chest, I still think it's weird the knife was left in." I checked my wristwatch. "Damn, I just realized the time, I have to run now to meet Nunez, but first I've got to check in with Mimmo and Mostly. Thanks, Amy, love you!"

"Love you too. Keep me posted. *Please!*"

"Don't worry, I'll email or wake you up again. *Ciao.*"

On my way down to the docks, I stopped in first at Fellini's to see Mimmo. Taking Mostly up to the Mirador was out of the question, so Mimmo decided he'd hang out at Fellini's to watch the movie, and then go home. I told him I was feeling better now, having spoken with Amy. I thought about her predicament on my short walk to the Once a Day.

Working high-profile murder cases and having your work challenged by well-paid, older men with serious reputations was not an easy situation for a young woman, even if you were brilliant and resilient like Amy. We chose separate paths when we went on for our doctorates. I knew my own nature and had directed my work to a more theoretical area, where I would be sheltered from the storms of unpredictable human interactions that normally Amy thrived on. But for some reason I was now ignoring my instincts and trying to emulate her.

On the dock, I walked through a cluster of old men playing dominoes at tables arranged outside on either side of the entrance to the bar. A halo of cigar smoke was suspended in the warm, moist air. They had long ago agreed to ignore the passing of strangers.

Inside, Nunez was waiting at a table, tactfully distant from the counter and isolated under the ceiling-hung television in the corner of the room. I noticed the small thermal cooler containing my egg evidence parked on a chair beside him. He looked even better than he had in his hospital greens. Now he wore a tan silk shirt, perfectly pressed blue jeans, and expensive leather loafers.

After a friendly greeting, he opened the conversation with a concise summary of the physical evidence. Apparently, Ballero had given him permission to speak freely with me. Why was the Chief Inspector so willing to include me in the investigation? Nunez frankly admitted that this surprised him as well.

"I think for one thing, he was really impressed by your quick assessment that the beach could not have been the murder scene. When my opinion backed that up, he understood your field of knowledge is enormously helpful in these circumstances."

"Thank you."

"But the second reason is not as flattering."

I braced myself.

"This is a very small town with many connections and more tensions than might be noticeable on the surface."

He paused to take a long drink from his beer.

"In my opinion, Ballero suspects this woman's murder is not a personal *chirpa*, that it may have a wider meaning, and needs to be truly resolved for the business interests of the community. Basically, he can use any help he can get. I think he's really puzzled."

Although we'd spoken a mix of Spanish and English at the morgue, we were now speaking English only to insure our privacy in the bar. At first, I did not understand his use of the Spanish word *chirpa*, so it took a few moments for me to realize the translation in English meant 'fluke.'

I was keenly interested in this point of view because from my little contact with Esmeralda, I felt in my gut that she was such an unlikely victim. She was a determined and strong person, and she had street smarts from running that nightclub. Whereas statistics show that most women are murdered by someone they know—often a man they've had some romantic or sexual contact with—that scenario just didn't jive with my opinion of her. Also, Nunez had found no signs of rape or recent sexual activity. To my greater surprise, I learned from Nunez that her preliminary blood work had revealed no alcohol or drugs. With the exception of the mortal wound in her back, there weren't any traces of violent bodily contact either. Only those delicate fragments of the natural world fixed in her hair could tell us how she had been taken so unawares.

I thought about the word Nunez used to describe the idea that she had been in some way unlucky, *chirpa*. This word must have come from the Greek root *"chir"* which meant "hand." I knew this from learning Greek and

Latin word roots while studying the taxonomy of insects—it made memorizing all the genus and species names easier.

Had Esmeralda had a *hand* in her own fate? Or was the only hand involved in her death the one that had held the knife?

Nunez's technician had been walking around town while we were talking, and now he rejoined us just as it was time to board the ferry. Nunez paid the bill. We walked out past the domino players and around the corner, and down the pier to where tourists were lined up ready to cross the gangway to the speedboat. The tourists fell roughly into two categories: the young, alternative types with towering backpacks, hiking boots or Velcro sandals, and the older, well-heeled Germans and Brits in shorts and sunhats, dragging their wheeled suitcases behind them.

A few of the latter were leaning on their recently purchased, hand-carved walking sticks, while others herded children carrying pails filled with shells and rocks or favorite toys. Nunez and his assistant looked suspiciously out of place in their street clothes carrying only briefcases and the cooler. But maybe it was just obvious to me, knowing as I did that their cooler was not for drinks.

7

As if my life were not complicated enough at the moment, I got a horrible surprise when I walked into the lounge at the Mirador for my meeting with Dr. Lopez. Sitting at the end of the sleek gleaming bar, admiring herself in the mirrored wall behind the bartender was the stone in my shoe, Strawberry Shortcake.

That wasn't her real name of course, but it was what I always called her in my mind and when I complained about her to Mimmo, who was obviously smitten with her extraordinary assets.

Strawberry Shortcake was a high-end Berlin hooker with a Russian handler. She had hair the texture of cotton candy, the most artificial red color imaginable, but everything else about her was 100 percent natural. I was in a good position to know, as we were both members of the same gym back in Berlin, a pricey haven of wellness and relaxation amidst the hustle-bustle of a busy shopping area. She had a jaw-dropping body that she draped over towels in the mixed sauna room with an animal-like lack of self-consciousness. What was so fascinating about her is how she managed to radiate pure sexuality and childish exuberance at the same time. She didn't look in the slightest way shopworn or damaged as did so many of the working girls parading around the Kurfürstenstraße in their trademark thigh-grabbing leather boots but otherwise minimalist attire. When she had clothes on, they were invariably in bright lollipop colors and made out of some soft, furry, clingy material, which made her resemble an over-sexed stuffed toy.

Her skin was a dewy opalescent white like the interior of a fresh magnolia blossom, and her blue-violet eyes were the color of forget-me-nots. She was stunningly beautiful. Her Russian boyfriend pimp, on the other hand, looked like a cross between Vladimir Putin and an Easter Island monolith. His eyes were so hard you could cut diamonds with them. She spoke German with that slurry Bavarian accent that I can barely understand; she'd clearly been raised on a dairy farm, somewhere with good nutrition and bad education. If she had known anything better, she'd have been selling herself in Hollywood, or trying for Germany's Next Top Model, or preferably not selling herself at all. She fascinated me so much I could almost overlook the fact she gave my husband a blowjob in the wine cellar of his restaurant before we were married.

But I couldn't.

Mimmo's *osteria* is a favorite destination for Berlin's elite. Contrary to the implication of its name, *La Strada* is in a renovated 19th century carriage house, tucked away in a hidden courtyard. Only personal references and a reservation get you directions. Famous politicians, movie stars, musicians and other prominent people sit elbow-to-elbow in a cozy room, eating and drinking family-style at long tables laden with fine linen and Italian ceramics, as if they were in Mimmo's tasteful rustic home in Italy.

In winter, their drivers and bodyguards pass the time around a fireplace in the front hall cloakroom, or in the good weather, in the attached garden that Mimmo tends himself. The bodyguards especially like *La Strada*, as there is only one way in and out of the double courtyard, and only a single entrance to the restaurant, and no windows at all.

Exactly how Strawberry Shortcake got to be a regular at *La Strada* was never very clear to me, something about a Russian bodyguard being friends with her pimp boyfriend. But in any case, during one very late-night party, my husband let himself be compromised against the premium years of *Brunello di Montalcino*, a fact that he unwisely disclosed to me later in the trusting honeymoon stage of our courtship, while he was under the renowned wine's influence.

I was stunned to see her here in front of me. *Of all the gin joint, in all the towns in all the world, she walks into mine?* What the hell was going on here?

Could this really be a coincidence? I panicked and looked around first for Mimmo and then for the boyfriend, but neither was in sight. She was cheerfully drinking alone, one of those girlie cocktails with lots of fruit and paper umbrellas. Before I could make up my mind how to handle the situation, she caught my reflection in the mirror and whirled around on her barstool, drink in hand, straw between plump, curvy, shimmering, collagen-free lips.

"Was für eine Überraschung! Wie geht's dir?" she greeted me in the familiar form of German. She had always gone out of her way to be friendly with me when we were thrown together in the sauna or at a Pilates

class. I never could tell whether or not she knew Mimmo had told me. In her cheerful, evidently completely amoral world it wasn't something to worry about. She was just like those puppies that frolic joyfully around and wag their tail right after they've peed on your foot.

Tonight she was wearing white leather Roman soldier sandals that laced up to her knees and a sleeveless, scoop neck, white cashmere mini that could have been a man's undershirt if it were made of cotton. Around her tiny waist was a gold and tangerine-enameled daisy chain belt (with matching dangly earrings). Her toe and fingernails were lacquered shiny tangerine as well, with diamond chip nail 'art' inlaid in the form of daisies on each nail. I suddenly thought of Esmeralda's square purple nails in the hospital morgue and of Dr. Lopez who might be somewhere in the restaurant waiting for me.

I glanced around at the other patrons, several of whom had their eyes riveted on Strawberry Shortcake. *Do they know she's a prostitute?* I was frantically thinking. *What if someone tells Ballero or Dr. Lopez she's a friend of mine?* This completely paranoid thought was racing around my brain, while I was casually explaining that Mimmo and I were vacationing here, staying above the harbor over the Café Sport. I volunteered this last bit of unnecessary information to demonstrate absolute confidence in my relationship. I then asked her bluntly what she was doing here.

"Das Gleiche," she answered coyly. Which meant basically fuck all, because we both knew she couldn't possibly be doing "the same" thing here as we were. Strawberry Shortcake wasn't roaming the island looking for bugs—or anything else that wasn't a male hominoid—in her platform hooker sandals that showed off her diamond-chipped toenails. She also wasn't heedlessly grilling her creamy skin in the blazing sun like my husband and the other northern European tourists. What exactly *was* she doing here? And where was her stone-faced handler?

Just at the moment I was contemplating plopping down on the empty stool next to her to try and wheedle it out of her, I spied the elderly Dr. Lopez coming through the front door with a small party of older local people. They were greeted by the *maitre d'* and escorted through the bar area into the main dining room. I excused myself from Strawberry and moved across the room towards Lopez, who was more dressed up than I had ever seen him—a jacket and a thin bolero tie held with a beautiful oval piece of jasper set in silver.

"Hola, Señor Lopez."

We shook hands and he introduced me to his friends as an American colleague that he must confer with briefly. His group greeted me politely, and then moved on to the spacious, glass-fronted terrace overlooking the gorge.

We sat down at a small cafe table in the corner of the lounge, and I could feel Strawberry staring at us, though I didn't dare look in her direction. I carefully pulled the glassine envelope from my bag and placed it in front of the old botanist. Dr. Lopez looked inside quickly, and then held the tiny crushed blossoms to his nose and pronounced definitively, "They belong to a laurel species, *Laurus azorica*, a tree with aromatic umbelliferous florets, found prevalently in the humid zone between 500 and 1500 meters."

He pointed out to me that as this species appeared more frequently than other laurel trees, I would need extraordinary luck with my katydid if we hoped to reduce a lot of territory to a searchable area where both plant and insect species overlapped. Still, the flowers alone provided us at least with one parameter: minimum elevation.

He pulled out a beaten up old Biro from his pants pocket and began flipping through his notes: delicate, elegant printing filled every line on every page. That previous summer, he recollected, two German graduate students had been in the Canary Islands doing a survey of Orthopteran species. He'd given them some assistance as well as permission to survey in the *Parque*. On returning to their University at Osnabrück, they had emailed him a letter of thanks. He was now passing on to me their names and email address, so that I could contact them about any Tettigoniidae species and vegetation associations they would have recorded on La Sirena and the other islands.

I thanked him profusely for his help and excused myself for disturbing his evening.

"My great pleasure," he responded graciously, rising to join his friends in the terrace room.

I glanced over in the direction of my redhead friend. She had vanished. The only trace of her was the paper umbrella opened, upside-down, plugging the mouth of her empty glass.

8

Monday morning when I woke up I knew something was wrong. I looked at the travel clock beside our bed. I'd slept three hours later than usual. Mostly hadn't tried to get me out of bed for his morning walk, and Mimmo, a dedicated night person who normally slept way past my rising, could be heard in the kitchen making cleaning noises and singing passionately along to an Italian opera. The room was still in relative darkness, thanks to the heavy curtains Esmeralda had hung on the windows. She'd decorated the apartments for her mother with accessories from the Ikea store on Tenerife. The sea green and navy blue drapes matched the coverlet on our bed. I lay in the cool darkness of the bedroom listening.

I recognized the aria as "Una furtive lagrima" from Donizetti's *L'Elisir d'Amore*. A hidden tear, one of the saddest songs I'd ever heard. I once asked Mimmo to translate the lyrics for me when we were at the opera in Berlin. He replied succinctly, "Love kills you," and went to the bar. I knew my husband. When he sang opera he was feeling sad; when he cleaned house energetically he was nervous. The combination was a lethal cocktail. I needed to feel my way carefully into our itinerary for the day.

Sunday's events had gathered momentum like a loose boulder rolling down an incline. I hadn't had any time to reflect or even eat properly the day before as I chased after the intangible truth about Esmeralda, and had been forced to confront my jealous fears.

Next, I thought about Udo sitting with me in communal silence on the stone steps as we waited for the police. I don't think I'd ever seen Udo in daylight before, only in the gloomy shadows of the Café Sport. He didn't look good. His skin was pasty, his dark hair thinning on top, and he had seemed even more spectral and ineffectual than when he was moving around behind the bar pouring drinks. Mimmo had overheard rumors at Fellini's that Udo had been seen having a loud, heated argument with Esmeralda on Friday afternoon at the entrance to her club.

I wanted to talk at length to Udo and find out what Mimmo and Ballero had discussed in the hospital garden. But first, I needed to find out what had set off my husband into this operatic cleaning session.

When I had returned late in the evening from my planned meeting with Juan Lopez at the Mirador and my shocking Strawberry Shortcake sighting, I was so emotionally and physically drained, I simply collapsed under a hot shower, crawled into bed and fell asleep almost immediately.

I appeared in the kitchen in my robe and slippers. Mostly ran up to me with that confused eagerness that dogs show when their daily routine has been violated.

"Well, I really overslept!" I said feeling guilty, wondering how to bring up the thorny news that Strawberry Shortcake had joined us on our vacation.

"You are on holidays, Epiphany!" Mimmo grumbled accusingly as he swept the kitchen floor with a dilapidated broom. "Sit down, I make your coffee. " He knew I sensed he was in a bad mood. "This is too much for you," he tacked on as an afterthought.

I watched as he filled the little metal basket of the espresso pot with the coffee especially bought from the one Italian-owned grocery store in town. He heated milk and whipped it with a battery-run hand gadget he always traveled with.

"What's happened, honey?" I asked gently. He just shrugged his shoulders and was silent. "Did you take Mostly for his walk?" I tried again.

"We saw Serenella on the road, so she came on the walk with us."

"Oh shit!" I knew now exactly what the problem was.

"What was she doing *out*?" I exclaimed. I thought if this had happened to me at her age, I would have stayed in my room, terrified of dealing with anyone.

"She was taking the trash out for her grandmother, and we saw her as we came up to that corner where the bins are, on our way to the cliff road, and she asked to come."

"Oh, God, what did you say to her?'

"Well, she was very dignified, for a child," Mimmo smiled despite himself. "Standing very straight. But her eyes had been crying. She asked where you were."

I groaned. "Did she know I was the one to find her mother?"

Mimmo nodded. "I told her you were still sleeping but she'd see you later." I nodded in agreement, wondering if she was going to ask me any questions that I couldn't bear to answer.

"She told me that Constanze Therese had gone to the church to talk to the priest, and there were lots of visitors at the house. She wanted to get out of there for a while, but she didn't want to see her girlfriends at their houses. So I suggested she come with Mostly and me, and we go on an adventure."

"An adventure? What kind of adventure?"

We hiked up that *barranco* behind the fruit farm. She'd never been up there. She said she was scared of the lizards, but I told her that with Mostly with us, no problem! He would scare away the lizards and I told her that you were a biologist and you knew everything about animals, and you promised me there weren't any lizards near to the ocean."

"What? I never said that..."

"I know, but the child wanted to come and I just wanted to make sure she could have a good time and relax."

"And was she okay do you think?"

Mimmo had been smiling when telling me his lizard story, but his expression shifted.

"I think she's really..." he searched for the word in English. "How do you say, traum...?"

"Traumatized."

I thought about the relation to the German word for dreaming, *träumen*. To be caught in a bad dream.

"Poor kid, her father drowns when she's a baby and then her mother is murdered," I said shaking my head, "my grandmother would have said,

55

'God has a special purpose for her.'"

Mimmo stared at me. This is where we often parted ways. Despite my training in science, I'd never completely discounted the Catholic religion of my childhood, so intertwined with my Mexican heritage. Yes, I had definite problems with its dogma, its positions on certain biological and moral issues, but I still found myself yearning for the comfort it once brought me, like the engulfing embraces from my loving *abuela* who still goes to Mass daily.

Mimmo, on the other hand, had lumped together the Catholic Church, the Mafia, Berlusconi, and the claustrophobic family dynamics of traditional Italy in one box, and tied it up neatly with the ribbon of the Italian communists he'd joined before dropping out of university. The whole package now sat somewhere in storage, where it waited to be sorted out in the distant future.

"My grandmother thought God gave tragedy in childhood as a test to strengthen your soul and bestow wisdom," I explained.

"I'll say that to Serenella the next time I see her," said Mimmo, raising one eyebrow. "She asked me when we were on our walk if I believed in God."

"Oh no. What did you say?" I couldn't have predicted what Mimmo would have said in such a moment.

"I said I believed that I was God, and so was Mostly and the ocean and the birds and everything that was living."

I could see what was coming next. "And then she asked me if I thought God was in the person who killed her mother." I remained speechless.

"So I say that I think, maybe, in such a person God disappears to our eyes, like the water on the beach at low tide, but there is always the chance it comes back. I tell her God has to be in everything he made, even in what to us is disgusting and bad."

I remained silent.

"What's the matter? Do you think I was wrong to say that?"

"No, no, not at all. It's just that you reminded me of something that happened when I was a child, and I haven't thought of it in all these years."

Mimmo started to make us more coffee.

"Do you remember I told you my mother's youngest brother was a priest? Well, we used to go occasionally on Sunday down to his parish for church, but it was about two hours south of where we lived, so we didn't go every Sunday. Anyway, after Mass, my parents took him out to lunch with us, and once he told me that during the Consecration of the bread and the wine, he noticed a fly drowned in the wine. But the fly was now sacred like the Body and Blood of Christ, because it had been part of the Consecration. It, too, had undergone the Transubstantiation—where the bread and wine really become the body and blood of Christ. So he didn't know what to do with it!"

Mimmo was smiling. "He should've just swallowed it. It was God too, no?"

I ignored him. "He took out the pin that holds that vestment the priest wears over his arm when he's saying Mass. He got the fly on the pin, and then he burned it in the flame of a candle on the altar. He said that's the only way you can get rid of something *so* sacred."

"He should have eaten it." I continued to ignore his comments.

"You'd think I would have remembered that time during those years I was pinning flies with Amy! It was only when you said God is in everything— *even what we find disgusting*—that I remembered it."

"Maybe that's why you do study flies, *amore*. Maybe you are really looking for God!"

It was just like Mimmo to make a joke that held more truth than I was prepared to hear.

Serenella had been the reason behind the opera singing, but the cleaning frenzy had a more alarming source, which took a little longer to uncover. Mimmo prepared my breakfast: ripe island bananas with milk, and a slice of the local goat cheese on toast.

I went out on our balcony, but all traces of the sun had disappeared leaving

Laurie Taylor

behind a sky crammed with grey clouds and a sultry, oppressive wind that sent small bits of trash skittering along the road below us. The beach was deserted despite the fact that the police had removed the crime scene tape at the steps. Clearly, Ballero did not expect to discover any more evidence in the black sand.

I decided to eat at the table inside our apartment.

Mimmo sat on the balcony smoking, looking mournfully at the empty overcast beach. He came back in the living room and announced, "I want to go back to Berlin as soon as we can get a flight."

Why?" I was astonished. "We rented the apartment until the end of the month. You don't have problems at the restaurant, do you?" I began to suspect that I wasn't the only one who knew about the sudden appearance of my rival.

"No, I just think the party's over," he waved his hand in the general direction of the beach and the harbor. "I don't want to be counseling a grieving child while you go playing policeman and putting yourself in danger."

"I think it's kind of nice that she trusted you to talk about it, and it sounded like you did the best you could."

Mimmo made a face.

"But your real problem is with me, isn't that so?" I asked.

"Epiphany, I think there's drugs somewhere in all this and I know about drug people—you don't. *Basta!* You're very smart about many things, but drug dealers are one kind of animal you know nothing about." Mimmo was waving his hands authoritatively, like a referee in a football match.

"What do you know? Something Esmeralda said to you before she died? Something someone else told you? *Tell me Mimmo*," I pleaded, "Tell me everything you know!"

I wasn't going to argue Mimmo's point that I'm not as street smart as he is. It was true. I'd never smoked hashish in Morocco or spent three months in a Spanish jail, when I was twenty for selling it. But I hadn't spent my whole life looking into a microscope either. I'd inhaled more than once when I'd been in college. My goal at the moment was not to compete with

58

my husband but to use him as a resource, because with his remarkable social skills one could certainly get more information out of the locals than a cop ever could.

"Was she dealing at the club?" I asked.

"No," he answered thoughtfully, "the interesting thing about Esmeralda was she liked a good time, but she never lost the real view. She wouldn't endanger her business, or Serenella's future, by getting mixed up with dealing."

"Then what makes you say that drugs are at the bottom of all this?"
"Something I heard at Fellini's."

"From who?"

"From Enzo."

I started to laugh. Enzo was one of the few Italians hanging out there who could speak pretty good English, although he always prefaced his contributions with: "You must excuse me, my English is not so good..." Enzo was a charming drunk. If Amy were going to cast him in our movie life, she would refer to him as Johnny Depp.

Enzo had beautiful, black, shoulder-length hair he wore tied back with a bandana in pirate fashion. He also had the same sort of dandy mannerisms as the actor, which suited his stylish Italian clothes—which he sometimes wore two or three days in a row when he was on a binge. His beautiful heiress wife had been killed in some awful freak accident in Italy, which ironically, left him financially secure enough to travel from one island to another looking for, in his words, "the Last Beach."

When he was sober, he once confessed to me that the first year after his wife died he went to India to volunteer at one of Mother Teresa's missions. Sadly, he found she was not a saint like everyone else in the world assumed. That revelation had further deepened his despair. He eventually left Calcutta for Goa to try the ecstasy parties and an easier path toward spirituality. Instead of shocking me with this apparent heresy, he rather endeared himself, as most people would never dare to offer such an opinion about Mother Teresa, especially in Spain or Italy.

"And what did Enzo tell you, and why would you believe him?"

"He told me drugs come here from Sicily as well as from North Africa, and the people who have the most chance to make money from the tourists want the drug trade here."

"But I don't understand, what does this have to do with Esmeralda if she didn't allow dealing in her club?"

"That's exactly the point. Her club would be the best place to make new contacts with buyers, no?"

I had to admit that was probably true. If you wanted drugs on vacation, you would of course expect to score with the right stranger at the only after-hours club.

"And why do you take Enzo seriously?"

"He may be an alcoholic, but he speaks the truth. He's so..." Mimmo searched for the right word. "So *disconnected*. I think he is half dead already. What's he got to lose by being real?"

"So your theory is that maybe she was killed by some Italian mafia because she didn't let them deal drugs in her club?" The skepticism in my voice was evident. Mimmo knitted together his thick arched eyebrows. They reminded me of two dark caterpillars meeting over the bridge of his beautiful Roman nose.

"I don't have any theories, Epiphany. I'm just an Italian restaurant owner, not an academic. I just smell drugs here, and I don't want you wandering in your naïve American dream into a world you know nothing about!"

I felt a not so unfamiliar angry frustration with him boiling up to the surface, now spiced with jealousy and suspicion.

"Mimmo you can go home today, or tomorrow, or whenever, I don't give a damn, but I'm staying here and seeing this through. I have a professional responsibility. Already, I have involved Dr. Nunez from Tenerife and Dr. Lopez from the *Parque* in my 'theories,' as you like to call them. By now, probably Concha Magna in Madrid is working on the eggs we sent her. This is not the *Gastronomie* world, where you drink a few glasses of wine and change your mind about the evening's menu!"

I was sinking low. Normally, I respected my husband's profession and would never imply that it was less interesting or important than my own, but I also knew how to intimidate him when I wanted, or when I needed to get my own way. Marriage was compromise to a certain point, but I couldn't compromise my integrity, my need to make decisions independent of his views.

"I can take care of myself, you know. How do you think I made it to age thirty-three before I met you, without you protecting me from my American innocence?"

"You were very lucky," he replied.

We rarely argued this intensely. Mostly was sensitive to the escalating tension in our voices. His ears were perked and he was looking up anxiously, first in my direction and then in Mimmo's. He hesitantly wagged his four-inch tail as though this attempt at communication could distract us from our conflict.

"Look," I said, "I just don't have time for this. The first forty-eight hours after the recovery of a body are the most crucial for getting the evidence to find and convict the perpetrator," I said self-importantly. I seemed to remember this fact from a criminology course I'd taken as an undergraduate, and it further strengthened my position against Mimmo's interference.

There was no clock in our kitchen and I'd left my wristwatch in the bathroom where I'd removed it when showering the night before. I looked at the position of the sun in the sky, faintly visible behind the profusion of clouds.

"I imagine I only have about 18 hours left, and I'm not going to waste them arguing with you."

I turned on my heel and went into the bedroom to get dressed.

When I re-emerged, I grabbed my backpack and keys off the kitchen counter.

"Where are you going now?" Mimmo shouted after me. Frustration infused his voice with the Italian machismo I had long ago learned to simply ignore.

"I'm going to get my nails done," I called back over my shoulder.

9

The only nail salon in town was located inside the *Palmer Canaria*, the expensive five-story hotel we'd carefully avoided upon our arrival. Built on an agricultural strip on the outskirts of town, it faced the main road running alongside the sea, surrounded by hectares of well-endowed banana trees on its other three sides. A rooftop swimming pool was the main attraction, though the architects had neglected to consider the wind factor at that height. Without a protective screen, sunbathers were provided with a stunning view at the price of the idiosyncrasies of the island weather.

I checked in at the reception desk and asked for directions to the salon, which I found on the ground floor tucked in between an over-priced gift shop and the bar lounge. There was only a manicurist and one other young woman cutting a client's hair towards the back of the shop. The manicurist was busy with a customer who looked all of twelve years old. She wore a cropped T-shirt exposing her flat pubescent belly and low cut tight jeans with a large glittery belt. I wondered if she might have been a friend of Serenella's, and then I thought of how either Esmeralda or her mother had managed to keep Serenella sheltered from the invasive values of MTV culture that seemed to be encroaching worldwide, even on remote islands such as these.

I asked for an appointment to get a new set of nails.

I'd had my nails done once before in my life, when I had to wear a formal gown to a fundraising event. My date was a Silicon Valley venture capitalist, not my usual type.

My cuticles had been dry and peeling from constant exposure to alcohol while handling and storing insects too small or soft-bodied to be pinned or pointed on a paper label; my nails were broken and ragged from sorting through soil samples. When I tried on my beautiful dress at a San Francisco store, I realized I felt a bit like Cinderella—and the Fairy Godmother's wand had somehow missed my hands.

Getting a set of nails you sit face to face, just inches away from a stranger for over an hour while she holds your hand. It's not a good profession for introverted people. I found that at the end of my hour I knew just about everything about my manicurist, her boyfriend and her problems with her sister, and she knew almost as much about me. If I were a regular customer, as I assumed Esmeralda had been, my entire personal history might be recoverable to someone skilled in diplomatic gossip.

We started by soaking both my hands in warm soapy water while Maria prepared her instruments. Then she showed me a large tray of nail polishes from which I was to choose a color. I looked thoroughly, searching for the frosty lilac color that I remembered from Esmeralda's lifeless hands. Yes, it was there, nestled in between a darker purple and a shocking pink. I pulled it out with one wet hand and examined the shade more carefully. I was almost sure it was the same color. I was relieved because I'd been worrying that this whole charade might have been in vain, and Esmeralda might have gotten her nails done privately with a girlfriend or someone else.

"I'd like this one," I said, watching her reaction.

Maria had unnaturally green eyes, lined in black, Cleopatra-style. They looked strangely out of context on an otherwise ordinary face with a large nose and small chin.

Her dark hair streaked with gold was tied in a knot at the base of her neck, and large gold hoop earrings dangled from her ears. I noticed that her nails were short and without color. She smiled at me politely when I selected the polish, but I thought I caught a shadow pass ever so fleetingly across those magnificent eyes.

She gently lifted my right hand from the soaking dish and began trimming my cuticles. My Spanish puzzled her. Her opening remark was: "Are you Cuban?"

"No," I explained, "Mexican American."

She looked faintly surprised. "We don't get many Americans here."

"I know, that's because the dollar is very low to the Euro right now, and Americans don't travel so much, anymore."

"Because of the war on terrorism?" she said it as a question.

"Well, yes, maybe." I replied. "But also, Americans just don't get around as much anyway, as say Germans, or the British. Did you know that only twenty-five percent of all Americans own a passport, that even George Bush didn't have a valid passport before he became president?"

While that was one of my favorite bits of trivia to drop into travel conversations, it didn't have the expected effect on Maria.

"Yes," she said, letting out a big sigh and poking painfully at my cuticles with a stick tipped in cotton. "These are not good times. It's not safe anywhere anymore."

Here was my opening.

"Even on this beautiful, peaceful island someone was murdered," I started out cautiously. To my surprise, Maria lay down the cuticle cutter and her stick on the white towel next to my hands, and tears welled up in her big green eyes.

"I'm sorry," she whispered as she looked around for a tissue. "She ... the person who was killed, she was my friend, well, one of my customers, and I still can't believe it!"

I took one of my wet hands, quickly wiped it on the towel, then reached over and patted her hand. "I'm so sorry, I shouldn't have mentioned it, how terrible!"

She was drying her eyes, and I sensed that she did want to talk about it.

"I knew her a little, actually, myself," I confessed. "Because we rented our apartment from her mother, and her daughter Serenella likes to play on the beach with our little dog." I found myself babbling, trying to find the fine line between being truthful with Maria while not giving myself away completely.

Of course, the mention of Serenella brought new tears to the surface. I couldn't help but like Maria, and I felt like a creep knowing I was only there to squeeze information from her.

"You know, I think she must have been a great mother," I said, "because Serenella is a lovely little girl." That was being honest, and it focused Maria on one positive detail.

She nodded her head in agreement and picked up my hand once again. The jabbing of my cuticles continued, and I tried to keep my alarm at the process from showing on my face.

"It must have been very hard being a single mother," I continued sympathetically. Maria nodded, "She came from a rich family, but still it's hard for a woman without a husband, and Constanze Therese is very domineering too, so her help came with a price tag. You know what I mean?"

"But I thought Esmeralda was pretty... why didn't she remarry after losing her husband? It seems that would have been the easiest course to take." I ventured.

"Not on this island," said Maria, a brief smile darting across her face.

"What do you mean?"

Maria sighed again. "Any man with some ambition gets the hell out of here ... they go to school in Tenerife, or on the mainland, and they don't come back. Esmeralda's husband Tomas was studying medicine in Madrid. He drowned here while they were back visiting on vacation. Look around you here..." Maria was holding a nail file and she made a small circle with it in the air for added emphasis, "What kind of young men do you see here?"

I was afraid to venture an opinion.

"Drunks and farmers." Her beautiful eyes rolled up in the direction of her perfectly plucked and penciled eyebrows. I checked her ring finger and saw that it was empty.

"What about foreigners?" I asked. "Please!" She laughed, "No girl in her right mind is going to marry a *German*." And then, I don't know what inspired me to ask my next question. "What about an Italian? My husband is Italian."

Maria stopped her filing for a minute. "Really? Well, I don't know about your husband, but the ones that we get here tend to be drug addicts, not all of them of course—Peppe at Fellini's is a good man. And Italians and Spanish people have more in common, but they do make up a lot of the drug crowd here."

I thought about the argument I had just gone through with Mimmo, and I felt unsettled.

"It's a numbers game," Maria continued, "I'm not saying every local guy is a drunk, a drug addict or a farmer, but when you think about how hard it is to even find some guy that you are attracted to—then our chances of finding the right man are really almost..."

"*Nada?*" I suggested.

"*Claro,*" she said. I thought about how Maria might have done in a statistics class if she'd had the opportunity to further her education. She was clearly very bright and perceptive, and as my nails slowly progressed, finger-by-finger, brush stroke by brush stroke, she painted a vivid socio-economic picture of the limited world within which she and Esmeralda had lived.

I learned from Maria that Constanze Therese had been the oldest daughter of a wealthy vineyard owner. When she was born, over fifty years ago, La Sirena was still an agrarian society, completely ignored by tourists who were only starting to discover the unspoiled beaches of Spain's Gold Coast and a few of the larger, more accessible islands in the Canarias. When Constanze's father died, he followed the traditional practice of primogeniture—which helped to concentrate the economic and political power in the hands of an elite class—and left all his land to her while she was still in her late teens. Her younger sister and her mother were entirely dependent on her for support.

The vineyard continued to be managed by one of her father's friends and business partners. Not surprisingly, several men courted Constanze Therese at once, including Esmeralda's father. Yet, despite her strict Catholic faith, Constanze Therese, who for a young woman had already experienced an unusual degree of power and independence, was not really keen on getting married when she found herself pregnant with Esmeralda. The baby's father disappeared to South America, and it was never clear who had abandoned whom.

In any case, Constanze Therese continued to flaunt convention, and losing interest in the grape-growing industry, she began selling off large pieces of her inheritance while buying up properties near the beaches. In the 70s, European hippies gave the island a reputation as a cheap paradise close to Africa, an alternative destination to the expanding concrete coastline along the European side of the Mediterranean. Eventually, more conventional tourism followed, people who still sought out intact nature but wanted a few fine restaurants and places to shop. Constanze Therese and a few other big landowners continued to break up and develop the property near the dry coast where holidaymakers wanted to be. In the late 70s, a major road was cut through the mountainous interior of the island, connecting villages and points of interest. But as climate directs the evolution of ecosystems, it also shapes social structure. It was only the southwestern face of the island that was blessed—or cursed, as some might say—by fairer weather.

Maria, born in the early 80s, was far too young to remember the old way of life. However, her father was a fisherman, and she'd grown up listening to his irritation and anxiety over the degradation he observed in both the ocean waters and the community life.

As I listened to her talk, it seemed to me that her emerald eyes were scanning for something: a clue to the future, an answer from the past. It was as though her friend's sudden death had cast her into a free fall from the great cliffs that sheltered the town. Her speech was rapid, and occasionally I had to ask her to repeat herself because her Sirenian dialect was still a challenge for me.

While her portrayal of Constanze Therese was sometimes less than flattering, I immediately understood two things.

The woman adored her daughter and granddaughter, even if mother and daughter butted heads more often than not.

Secondly, while Esmeralda was working hard to gain her independence, she followed in her mother's footsteps, thumbing her nose at community expectations. She joined the German women topless on the beach, both literally and metaphorically. In short, after recovering from a long depression following the death of her husband, Esmeralda conducted her life like a man.

As for her love life, she'd had one major relationship that lasted a few years. Her boyfriend was stationed on La Sirena in the Guardia Civil, but had returned to Sevilla after his assignment. Maria wasn't the first person to explain to me that it was official policy to rotate officers on the islands in an attempt to keep them impervious to local corruption. But Maria acknowledged that even so, some of the young men were known to ignore drug dealing because of their own fondness for smoking hashish.

"What about Esmeralda's ex-boyfriend?" I asked. "Was he like that do you think? And why didn't their relationship continue after he was transferred?"

"No, he wasn't corrupt, at least not from how she talked about him, I don't think so. The problem was that when it was time for him to be transferred, Esmeralda couldn't see taking her daughter away from her grandmother and everything she'd always known and having her live in a big city. Also, she'd invested so much in getting the bar up and running; she couldn't just walk away from it! Some people in town had tried to stop the disco from opening but she outwitted them."

My ears perked up. The more I heard about Esmeralda, the more I liked her, and the more determined I was becoming to find out who had taken her life.

"How did she outwit them?"

"She'd put all her money into renovating the warehouse. It hadn't been used at all since the tuna fishing industry disappeared. Just before she was to open, they passed a new fire code specifying the height of the ceiling should be more than a certain number of meters if the occupancy capacity was over seventy-five persons. That was a meter over the height of her existing ceiling, and they knew it was too expensive for her to raise the roof. She couldn't make a profit unless she had at least one hundred people in there on weekend nights."

"So what did she do?"

Maria laughed at the memory of what she was about to tell me. "She paid some illegal immigrants next to nothing to go in and break up the concrete floor and carry away the pieces. Then they dug out the earth for a meter or so, laid a new floor and built steps down from the street level!"

I remembered how when I first entered Esmeralda's club, I'd thought it unusual that it had a basement feeling, unlike anything else I'd seen in town. I had thought that it made the place more interesting, giving it a kind of city quality.

"Who were these people who didn't want her club?" I pressed on.

"A mix of folks, actually. Some were bar owners who feared that

69

customers would leave their own bars earlier to head to Esmeralda's for the action. Others were conservative people who thought having a dance place would bring in more 'hippies', she smiled again. "They still call them that here, like we were still in the 70s or something. They thought it would encourage more of the drug crowd."

"Do you think someone would *kill* her because of the club?" I couldn't help myself from asking Maria outright.

Maria stopped delicately working on my pinkie finger and paused to think. In my head I heard Amy's voice over the telephone, "It's *something emotional!*"

"She was kind of stressed for about a month before she died. I remember we had two nail appointments where she was really smoking a lot, like she had to have one hand free all the time so she could smoke."

"Was it something to do with the club then?"

An odd expression came over Maria's face. "Well it's kind of bizarre, now that I think about it ... I remember her exact words were, 'You know Maria, I think my business is killing me.' I know people say stuff like that all the time, but she seemed so..." Maria searched for the right word, "... *resigned*, like she was kind of defeated, like giving up the fight."

"What fight?" Maria hesitated.

I wanted to confide in her that I was actively working with the police to solve her murder, but I knew that I didn't dare reveal my position to anyone except Dr. Lopez at the *Parque*, who could be trusted to keep my involvement under wraps.

"I think it was just the whole atmosphere she had to deal with all the time," Maria started out slowly, as though with each word she was measuring carefully how faithful she was being to her friend's memory. "First of all, the drinking. She knew she was drinking too much, but it's hard to be in that kind of place all night drinking Fanta, while everyone is getting all happy and rowdy around you, I guess."

I nodded my head in agreement, trying to get more out of her.

But I think it was more that people were pressuring her from all sides. She felt guilty that she wasn't at home with her daughter at night, and she was afraid she was losing her influence to Constanze Therese. Then there were just all the people she had to deal with all night."

She paused and tipped her head to one side, as if listening to something that only she could hear.

"I mean she had Busta, you know that big guy who works the door and throws out the trouble, but when it came down to it, everything was her responsibility: hiring the bands and the DJs, dealing with the liquor companies and the delivery men, everything. She had some hired help, but she always said you could never rely on anyone, really, and she did have one bartender she caught stealing."

"Stealing? Was that recently?"

"No, it was when her boyfriend was here. He offered the bartender a deal—repay the money in exchange for no police involvement. So he got off easy. Anyway, I knew that guy and he wasn't a killer, if that's what you were thinking. In fact, Esmeralda was more hurt than angry, because she'd looked on the guy as a friend and had been nice to him as an employer, you know, giving him time off when he had problems, that kind of thing."

I nodded my head in sympathy. I was getting fonder of Esmeralda with each new revelation.

By now my right hand was in the ultra violet light machine, quick-drying, and Maria was putting the finishing touches on my left. I had to go for the final push.

"So you don't think there was something in particular going on this last month, something more than just getting tired with all the pressures?"

"Well, yes, there was something, something that had her rethinking her whole life—like all her major decisions. You know what she said to me?"

I was hanging on every word.

"She said, 'In another month, I'll be thirty, and I've really worked hard to be my own person, and now I find out I know nothing at all. I was wrong about almost everything, and it doesn't matter what I do because my life is turning out just like *hers*. I'm becoming my mother!'"

"In what way?" I realized I was barely concealing my eagerness. "*How* was she becoming Constanze Therese?"

Maria's eyes were filled with compassion.

"I don't know," she said miserably. "She wouldn't tell me, she just said it was a secret that she couldn't talk about with anyone, even me—and we were really close. We really were." Maria looked for the tissue box again.

"She didn't even get to her thirtieth birthday!" She wailed into the tissue. Her smudged mascara left a scattering of round black dots on the arc of her eye bone, making me think of the elytra of a ladybug.

10

I walked across the road to the sea wall, placed my backpack on it, and climbed up to think about what I had just learned from Maria. The wind whipped my long hair against my face. Below, the unusually turbulent sea rolled smooth oval-shaped stones against each other, sucking down trails of flotsam from the surface of the water.

As the waves retreated into the sea, all the rocks clattered backwards and under, leaving behind only a bright necklace of assorted plastic bits to mark the tide line. I liked the noise but it reminded me of something sad, or maybe it was just the sight of all that floating ocean garbage that was getting me down. For several minutes, I sat in the wind, listening to the breakers, the stones, and my own disconnected thoughts. I kept hearing Maria's voice speaking for Esmeralda:

My business is killing me.

I'm becoming my mother.

Why did these two things seem like clues to me? They could have meant anything at all, but my intuition told me they were more than ordinary complaining. What was Esmeralda's secret? What was agitating her to chain smoke during her last nail sessions?

Do you need the motive to solve a murder? Legally, *no* and it seemed to me that a motive was the one aspect of a murder that remained strangely indivisible by numbers.

It was the search for the square root of 2 that revealed to the Greeks that some things could never be expressed by a number; a diagonal and the side of a square are simply incommensurable. From their profound shock at this irrefutable fact, the word "irrational" came into our language, meaning essentially that number and reason is *not* the same thing. Sometimes reason is irrational. Yet, there was some drive within man, and within me for sure, that yearned for complete order.

As a scientist, one is trained to believe that life can be described by mathematics. Maybe that sounds cold and uninteresting to some people— to a poet or an artist—someone who is in love with words, or light, or color. That was how I was until I was twelve years old, when I found out what numbers really were.

I hadn't been able to see it in my first algebra class; it seemed like a lot of work for nothing. But in geometry when I could really see things: circles, triangles, and trapezoids—and how they related to what the numbers were saying—I realized mathematics was a language that explained relationships, and that all those relationships make up the structure of the entire physical world.

With numbers you could find the missing components of any system. You could know why the evening is dark, and even how much smaller the universe will be when all the stars start to evaporate and the night sky is as bright as the surface of our sun.

Yes, in the end it is hard to say what it all means. Math is so awesome and seductive, but what can you ever really know?

Could the truth of how a life came to be taken be described by mathematical relationships? It was a strange thought. In this case, the height of the assailant, the rate of velocity with which the knife descended, the angle of the knife, the width and the length of the blade, the ratio of the victim's muscle mass to the area of penetration. So many numbers coming together randomly, but perfectly to terminate a life.

Numbers certainly tell us what could *not* have occurred, but do they tell us what really did happen? How far beyond the power of numbers does the truth reach? I felt I needed both the power of numbers and a manicurist's feminine insight to find out.

I looked at my watch. I had twenty minutes to get to the Internet place before siesta. It was shocking to me, coming from California's twenty-four hour society, that consumer life still followed tradition here and came to a halt for three hours in the afternoon, the narrow winding streets deserted, all the shops and even many of the bars and restaurants locked and shuttered.

It was ten minutes to three when I got settled on a cushion in the corner of the Internet room with my laptop up and running. I logged on to my email. There were several new messages, but only three of interest: one from

Concha Magna, one from Dr. Lopez, and one from Amy. I opened Concha's first.

Nunez had gotten the frozen eggs to her late Sunday evening and blessedly, she'd run the allozyme gels for us almost immediately. Allozymes are proteins encoded by structural genes made up of amino acids, some of which are electrically charged. Different species have different amino acid chains making up their proteins, giving them a particular net electrical charge. When the sample protein is prepared and added to a cellulose acetate gel, the electrical charge affects how quickly the proteins move through the polarized field, enabling us to identify their make-up. Whether a protein is extracted from an adult, a larva, or from a cluster of eggs, it will present the unique allozyme profile of its species. This is extremely important for identification of immatures, which have few distinguishing morphological characteristics. In other words, closely related maggots look pretty much alike!

In her Madrid laboratory, Concha had successfully compared our eggs to her profiles of adult species of all flesh-eating flies known in the Canary Islands, and the egg samples matched the *Calliphora vincia* adult profiles in her archive. The second sample I'd found slightly deeper in the wound had shown signs of eclosion, which meant that it was a bit older than the first sample and on the verge of changing from an egg to the first instar of a maggot.

All this was very good news for our investigation, giving us legal evidence for designating both the maximum and minimum intervals possible from the moment Esmeralda died to the time I found her. Now all I needed was the climate data from the weather station for that weekend and I could assess the time of her death more closely.

I hastily wrote a thank you letter to Concha. She'd also sent on a more official report to Nunez. I had five minutes left to scan Dr. Lopez's message. Amy would have to wait until tomorrow.

Dr. Lopez had forwarded me the German graduate students' letter to him about the results of their survey on La Sirena. I hurriedly emailed them Mimmo's phone number, explaining why we needed information and asking them to contact me as soon as possible.

The owner of *Uno Mundo* was impatiently waiting for me to log off as I was his last customer and he was more than ready to close the metal gate that cosseted his business for siesta. I packed up my laptop, thanked him, and hurried out into the empty street.

Mimmo's threat to return early to Berlin was now weighing heavily on my mind. I had to face him and work it out. I could hardly imagine him leaving Mostly and me behind on the island working a murder investigation without him. But he'd been really upset with me, and I'd been pretty flip with him, which is, I admit, not the high road out of a difference of opinions when you're in a relationship. Well, he wasn't going to be found on the beach in this weather, and the travel bureau was closed along with everything else, so the logical step would be looking in at Fellini's, where he was probably helping Peppe prepare vegetables for the evening's pizzas.

As I turned down the little alley leading to Fellini's, I was dismayed by the sight of Mostly sitting in the shelter of a large wine barrel which propped open the old wooden door at the threshold of the restaurant. He was anxiously on the lookout for me. When he saw me rounding the corner, he bounded up the alley with relief and exuberance, making me feel even worse about my fight with Mimmo. In one leap, he was in my arms, covering my face with kisses.

Mimmo was sitting at the counter with Enzo, talking with Peppe and Lola who were working in the small area behind the counter and in the kitchen. I sensed immediately that something was wrong, as all four of them looked up at me with more interest than was normal. I couldn't read whether Mimmo was still upset with me. I wondered if he'd been discussing his intention to leave the island.

"Udo's been taken to the jail for Esmeralda's murder," Mimmo announced dramatically.

"What?" I was so surprised I almost dropped Mostly.

"La Guardia come and take him away from the Sport, some hours past," said Enzo in his less-than-perfect English.

As my gaze shifted to Peppe and Lola, they just nodded their heads in silent confirmation. Peppe pulled down the Ramazotti bottle from the shelf behind him and poured me a glass.

"How do you know this?" I settled myself on the stool next to my husband, transferring Mostly to Mimmo's lap and then taking off my backpack.

"We were there," offered Enzo.

"When they came into the Sport," Mimmo chimed in, "I had to close the bar for Udo. He gave me the key."

I looked more closely at Mimmo trying to assess how long he'd been drinking with Enzo, who actually looked better than I'd seen him recently, clean-shaven, and very much the casual Italian fashion plate—Gucci loafers with no socks.

I remembered how crucial it was to cover my own interests in the case. I took a long swallow of my drink.

"How did he take it?" I asked, "Did he freak out?"

"I thought he was going to pass out," said Mimmo. "He went white in the face."

"This is a terrible mistake. There's no way Udo killed Esmeralda!" I said, aghast that Ballero had moved so hastily in the wrong direction. I couldn't understand why he hadn't waited for the forensic evidence we were working on. I couldn't imagine what was motivating him.

"Did they take him for questioning, or did they really charge him for the murder?"

Mimmo answered hesitantly.

"Well, they were speaking Spanish to him, so Enzo and I were not exactly sure if he was being charged, but according to Peppe, it doesn't matter because they can hold you in jail here for a few days without a charge before sending you on to the prison in Tenerife."

I looked at Peppe. He clearly didn't understand what Mimmo had just said in English. I asked him in Spanish how it was possible a person could be held without a formal charge. He explained it was a recent amendment to Spanish law, allowing the police more room to maneuver in dealing with terrorism. Although on this island they could pretty well do whatever they wanted anyway.

"Don't worry," said Mimmo, trying to reassure me, "He'll get a lawyer who can speak both Spanish and German."

I was so exasperated; I didn't know where to begin. "Look, there is *no* way that Udo could've killed Esmeralda..."

Peppe interrupted, "He was seen having a screaming fight with her Friday night, outside her place. He followed her out of the Sport and was shouting at her at the entrance to her club."

"Well, I've screamed at Mimmo more than once, myself, and I never killed him!"

That broke the tension a little and everyone laughed including my husband.

Then, Lola, who normally held back and let Peppe hold center stage, jumped into the fray, "Of course they're going to pin it on a foreigner if at all possible, especially a German!" She flapped her dishtowel in the air to give her opinion more emphasis.

Peppe who, despite his good nature, seemed to always play the skeptic in this type of conversation, asked, "How can you be so positive that Udo didn't just lose his cool and kill her?" He leaned forward resting his muscular arms on the counter in front of me, interlacing his sausage fingers together in a two-handed fist.

I looked at Mimmo. "Do you remember the day we were in the Sport a few weeks ago, and Mostly found that spider?" I turned to the other three and explained. "There was this really big brown spider crawling on the floor, and Mostly goes crazy with insects when they're moving. He has this instinct to get them in his mouth. I was afraid it might hurt him, and I pulled him back, and Udo came over with a glass and a beer coaster and caught the spider and put it outside."

Everyone remained silently looking at me.

"Don't you get it? A person who saves spiders instead of crushing them under their shoe doesn't plan to kill someone, lure them into the woods and stab them in the back!" It took me about three seconds to realize I'd said a lot more than I should have.

"What do you mean," responded Enzo in Italian, "She died on the beach, no?" Mimmo jumped in to save me, "'In the woods' is an English *figura retorica*. She *thinks* someone

thought about killing her, beach or no beach."

I was going to have to extract myself from my own slip of the tongue.

"Look, you all know I found Esmeralda, and I saw the knife in her back. It was weird, not a pocketknife or a type of knife a person would be carrying around. It was like a dagger or something. She was only stabbed once, a mortal wound. No impassioned thrusting around. Someone thought about what they were doing. So all I'm saying is that it doesn't fit with Udo. I just used the example of the spider to say he's basically a gentle soul. *He's not a cold-blooded murderer!*"

"*Basta!*" agreed Mimmo. At that moment, his cell phone rang. He answered and switched in to German, "*Ein Augenblick bitte.*" and handed the phone over to me. I thought it might be a friend from Berlin, but then I realized it was one of the entomology students from Osnabrück. I stepped away from the bar and out into the alley to talk with her. She'd been working online when my email had come through and called immediately. I thanked her, explaining again why and what we needed to know.

Like most graduate students, she was bubbling with enthusiasm to talk to someone about her work. The idea that it might actually be of some help in a murder investigation was making her day. She told me that they'd only found three species from the family Tettigoniidae on the island, two of them in the dry cultivated zone under 500 meters, and one, *Platycleis sabulosa*, had been recorded only in a wetter area on the southeastern outskirts of the protected park boundary. This species was also larger than the other two by several centimeters, so identification by the leg might be possible. She agreed to email me all three species descriptions, which would allow me to compare the ratio of leg-to-body measurements. She went on to confirm that the species seemed clearly associated with a particular type of dense grass vegetation that provided its seed diet.

I was elated by this news, as it meant I could rule out the other two species. The *Laurus azorica* blossoms that Dr. Lopez had so easily identified could also only be found at the higher moisture zone. Armed with this new information, I could go to Dr. Lopez's office and look at his GIS vegetation distribution maps, and find where *Laurus azorica* trees and the *Platycleis saubulosa*'s dense grasses possibly occurred together.

From my previous hikes up there searching for *Carabidae* beetles, I remembered that general location as a degraded site, with some scattered development and a few rough roads for vehicular access. It was within the realm of possibility that the murder had transpired up there, and the body was brought down during the night to the beach where I found it shortly after dawn. After some more casual entomology chitchat with my new acquaintance at the University at Osnabrück, I thanked her and hurried back inside the bar.

"That was my colleague at the Museum," I explained, lying for the benefit of my audience. "There's a mistake on one of our projects," I scooped up my backpack and Mostly at the same time, "So I have to go and do some math homework! *Ciao* everyone..." I ignored the concerned look on Mimmo's face, kissed him on the cheek and headed out the door. I was just hoping that when I had the weather data from the German trekking station, I could do my calculations and Udo would have a tight alibi for the time of the murder.

As I walked across the docks towards the beach, I thought about how Mimmo had looked at me as I left the pizzeria. Things were not good between us and I knew exactly what the problem was. People think that because I'm Mexican and he's Italian that we should have similar temperaments because we are both Latin types, but this is an oversimplification. For one thing, my culture's heritage is the dynamic between indigenous people and their conquerors—the Spanish. Italians were always the conquerors. They think their food, art, architecture and literature is the pinnacle of achievement and that in this respect most of the world worships at their feet. They're just a little bit arrogant in my book, while Mexicans are just a little melancholic with a wild streak. I could see these blueprints in both of us. I feel like Mimmo's attempts to rein me in just drive me further into unpredictable, sometimes even irrational behavior.

It was always there between us, but you never pay attention to the red light when you first fall madly in love, and by the time you come up for air there's a ring on your finger and your life is all tangled up in blue.

Why wasn't I willing to go home to Berlin like he wanted? Why did I have to go deeper into this tragedy, sticking my neck out and my nose into other people's business? Sometimes I didn't understand even myself, let alone our marriage. I walked through the boatyard and down the ramp to the beach.

I walked past the few people braving the changing weather, scattered on towels and blankets and children digging in the wet sand at the water's edge. I walked past an older Italian I knew from Fellini's, twisted in a yoga position on a straw mat. I walked to the farthest point where the beach disappears into the cliff face.

I needed some vigorous exercise to chase away the gloomy thoughts pulling me down. I stripped off all my clothes and weighted them down with my backpack. No one was in the water. The wind was whipping up wave action.

The water was cold at first, but I knew it would be only minutes before I became acclimated. I have spent most of my life swimming in the cold Pacific Ocean, surfing without a wetsuit more often than not. After the first three minutes, I go into a pleasurable numb space where I can stay in the water for hours. I breast stroked towards the horizon. The cries of the swifts circling the cliff wall became fainter and fainter as I gained distance from the shore.

I counted each stroke. When I'm nervous or anxious I count automatically without even thinking about it. I count anything, just like the Count on *Sesame Street*. I think it means that I'm a little obsessive-compulsive. But most entomologists are. It would drive normal people crazy to count the veins in a fly's wing, to measure the length of the hairs on a caterpillar.

Thirty-two, thirty-three, thirty-four, thirty-five, thirty-six. I saw a dinghy about thirty meters from where I had just surfaced. I decided to test my lungpower. I breathed in deeply, surface-dived underwater, and headed in the direction of the dinghy, counting.

Fifty-six, fifty-seven, fifty-eight, fifty-nine, I kept my eyes open underwater, my arms digging the water in perfect synchronization with my frog kick. My lungs began the slow burn. Eventually, I saw the silver hull of the boat, a blurry, light presence in the dusky green water. *I won't surface until I can touch it*, I promised myself. *Sixty-five, sixty-seven, sixty-eight. Just a little more, you can do it.*

Seventy, seventy-one, I burst through the surface of the water, sucking in sweet air, hooking my right arm over the rim of the boat, panting. Holding on with both hands, breathing a little less desperately, I looked straight down into a face: the eyes eaten by birds, rust-brown, blood-encrusted holes, a tangle of ropey red hair.

Strawberry Shortcake was sprawled on her back, one arm behind her head, the other akimbo, magnolia skin bruised, her white t-shirt dress pasted on her body with blood, and on her throat a big black beard was moving.

11

I kept up my crazy counting as I swam as fast as I could away from the boat and its grisly cargo. My heart was banging inside my rib cage and I could hear the blood pounding in my ears. I stopped to tread water until I felt calm enough to continue swimming.

Eighty-five, eighty-six, *this can't be happening to me,* eighty-eight, eighty-nine, two bodies, eighty- seven, in twenty-four hours, not possible, astronomical odds, finding two bodies, people I know, they'll never believe me, fingerprints, my fingerprints on the side of the boat, wet.

Can wet fingers leave prints? I don't know. Why don't I know that? Did anyone see me from the shore? Too far away maybe? No one looking... Mimmo. Why didn't I tell him I saw her earlier? We can leave? Get on the ferry as quickly as possible. Back safely in Berlin, no one knows. He'll be happy to leave. He doesn't have to know anything.

She was a hooker, just a hooker; she was bound to end up like this. It was just a matter of time. It's not my fault. I don't have to save the world.

Breathe, breathe, float on your back, float calmly, breathe slowly.

Think, think! Don't panic ... breathe, breathe ... the beard, so many of them, so far from the garbage bins on the docks, the color of her skin, blood, there was dried blood all over her shoulders, her chest.

I think.

I can't remember exactly.

Her throat was cut ear to ear! How long? How many hours was she lying out there?

He must have killed her in the boat, taken her for a romantic row, late last night, pulled her close and slit her throat from behind.

I already knew it was him— that mean-faced Russki. Where was he now?

I floated some more, my heartbeat gradually slowing down.

I felt a surprising grief for her.

I had a memory of us lying side by side on heated loungers in the tepidarium at our spa on Hauptstraße.

A tepidarium, a climate-controlled room is an Italian invention, good for people living in cold places with ungodly long winters like Berlin. The walls of our room were painted *trompe d'oeil* with a scene from the Italian Riviera. The beach on the walls blended into real sand on the floor scattered with real rocks, plants, and little lighted pools of water.

I could see her perfectly proportioned long legs, one stretched out full length, the other bent at the knee. I could see the small, heart-shaped tuft of pubic hair dyed red to match the color of her long hair which was, at that moment, wrapped in a thick white towel. She was reading a magazine propped against her thigh.

I was—as was usual around her—feeling brown-skinned, too big, too plain. She looked over at me and asked, "Can you read German?"

I nodded uncertainly. I figured she was reading a fashion magazine, not *Der Spiegel* or anything too difficult.

She handed across the page she was looking at to me. "Can you read me what it says under that photo?" She pleaded like a child. *"Bitte."*

Then seeing the expression of bewilderment on my face, she added apologetically, "I can't read, but I really want to know what's going on there." She pointed with a bejeweled nail at a photo of people in the Arctic clubbing baby seals.

It wasn't a fashion mag; it actually was *Der Spiegel*. The photo was in an article about Greenpeace and their relationship with the German coalition government. I read the text out loud as best I could. She nodded her turbaned head and appeared to be deep in thought.

"I only wear fake fur coats," she finally said, her tone matter of fact.

It made me really sad thinking about it, floating as I was not far from where she lay slaughtered almost as brutally as the baby seals.

Then suddenly an insight zinged through me like I had touched an electric eel. Strawberry Shortcake was illiterate, an '*Analphabetin*', as they are called in Germany. But how could she have grown up in southern Germany and have never gone to school? Bavaria is the heart of law-abiding, conservative *Deutschland* and the law that every child must be enrolled in school is strictly enforced. A child has to really be hidden away, *off the books*, to escape the attention of the authorities.

The answer to my question was obvious in hindsight.

Something terrible happened to her as a child. A dark history lay at the heart of her indiscriminate sexuality, her pedophile Lolita appeal. Strawberry Shortcake never chose the life she led, any more than she chose her death.

I stopped my dead man's float, and began methodically treading water again.

I was in a cold rage, deeper and colder than the Atlantic Ocean enveloping me.

I was going to get that bastard and nail him to the wall, that gimlet-eyed, Putin-faced fucker, and I was going to get Esmeralda's killer as well. SCREW MIMMO and SCREW BALLERO, and all the stupid men in the world who walk around like they own everything. THEY DON'T KNOW ANYTHING. They think with their dicks. That's why we've got this crazy world!

Testosterone in shoes and I'm just *sick* of them. THEY DON'T OWN ME.

I've got a goddamn good brain and I'm going to use it. A problematic God, or dumb luck, gave me chances these women never had. I can do this. I can do this! Amy will help me. *No one is going to get in my way.*

I put my face back in the water and began a rapid overhead crawl toward the shore.

On the beach once again I realized no one could have seen me for the brief moments I had surfaced so far away at the dinghy. The weather was now so overcast that almost everyone who had been there earlier had already gone home.

I shivered in the wind pulling my dry clothes on over my dripping wet body, and tried wringing the water from my long hair with my trembling hands. I looked a state, but I had to get to Ballero as quickly as possible. I'd take a taxi up on the docks.

12

Ballero listened to my story with polite disbelief. In the short ride to the town's police station, which was across from the bus station in the middle of town, I'd had time to decide exactly how much of my background with Strawberry I was going to reveal. I wasn't going to mention anything about Mimmo and his restaurant.

When I finished my short spiel about my swim, the discovery inside the dinghy, and how I suspected she'd been killed by her pimp boyfriend, whom I'd actually never seen on the island, the policeman wagged his head side to side while drawing deeply from his cigarette.

"Dr. Jerome, how can you know all about this woman, and you can't even tell me her name, her Christian given name?"

This seemed a logical question at first and stopped me in my tracks, but only for a moment. I realized Ballero's perspective came from his provincial life experience. Though he was at least twenty years older than me, he'd never lived anywhere but a place where everyone knew who he was.

"If we at least knew her name, we could check for her passport details on the passenger lists from the ferry line. We could start looking at the hotel registrations," he continued. Maybe he sensed I was withholding something from him, but it certainly wasn't her name.

"Chief Inspector, when a person lives in a very large city, a capital city, it's quite normal to have acquaintances, people you see regularly, but only because your paths cross in public places, because your schedules are similar. You might never formally introduce yourself, or maybe once, but you don't remember the name. Still, you become intimate in a way, just by repetition of exposure. Especially women, it's our nature to talk, and she and I were in a health club, half-naked most of the time. We shared about our lives and this is *what I know*. She had sex for money with men... rich men, not anyone who picked her up on the street, and she had a Russian pimp. I saw him several times when he was waiting for her downstairs in the reception area of the club lounge."

This was a bold-faced lie.

I saw him mostly at my husband's restaurant, but I wasn't going to open up that line of inquiry.

Ballero reached across his tidy and surprisingly empty desk, grabbed his big retro telephone and began ordering people around.

He requested the coroner and an ambulance to go down to the docks. He called Tenerife and got Nunez on the line, requesting his return on the evening boat to handle the autopsy.

Small beads of sweat began to form above Ballero's bushy brows. It was then that I realized he thought he might have a serial killer on his hands. In a space of two days, on an island that had very rarely seen suspicious deaths, two young women had been slain with a knife, one on the beach and one on a dinghy offshore. This second hasty conclusion would only prove his first had been erroneous. Udo was safely incarcerated at the time of Strawberry's murder, so if it was the same killer it certainly couldn't have been Udo. I knew the Chief was wrong on both counts. Udo was no killer and Putin-face was, and the Ruskie had no motive to kill Esmeralda. Hers was a very personal murder. Of that I was sure.

But I couldn't say anything.

I'd have to wait for Nunez to step in with his expertise. Maybe he'd be able to offer something tangible at this point in time.

I couldn't.

Meanwhile, I had to help Ballero understand who Strawberry really was, and help him find her real killer quickly, *really quickly*. If that bastard was still on the island and he recognized me, knowing I could lead the police straight to him I would, in all probability, be the third body to turn up on Nunez's table.

According to my grandmother, everything bad comes in threes.

I pulled my wallet out of my backpack and shuffled through my plastic. I found what I was looking for and placed a card in front of Ballero.

"Here's my membership card to Ars Vitalis," I said, "The phone number is on the back. Call and ask to speak to Kristin, she's the membership director. She can give you her real name. Just say the beautiful girl with white skin and bright red hair; she'll know exactly who you mean. Everyone knows her. Use my name, tell her I suggested her for the information." I saw a look of discomfort pass over Ballero's face.

"I can do it if you think your English isn't good enough," I tacked on.

He dialed the number, then handed me the phone.

We were lucky. One of the trainers I knew answered the phone. I asked to speak to Kristin, telling him it was urgent.

When she got on the line, I apologized for disturbing her. I described Strawberry and made up a story of how I needed her name because I'd forgotten it and we'd arranged to go to a musical together later in the evening. I'd bought the tickets ahead of time and was leaving one at the box office for her because I was going to be a bit late getting there. I didn't want her waiting for me.

It was a good thing Ballero didn't understand English, or he would have seen what a smooth and convincing liar I can be.

Kristin was initially a bit reticent, as Germans can be when you ask for something even just a little bit out of the ordinary, but eventually she got with the program and gave me the name: Dora Hoch.

Dora Hoch with diamond nails, born in Bavaria and dead at barely twenty in a blood-spattered dinghy with kites pecking her beautiful blue eyes out and her throat covered in flies.

I thanked her and hung up.

I took out a paper and my address book from my bag and wrote her name down on the paper. I wrote, 'Dora Hoch, Birthplace: Bavaria? Age: Around twenty?' I then opened my address book and transferred another name and number to the paper.

"This is the name of someone I know who works in the forensic-medico-legal wing of the Berlin *Kriminalpolizei*. He's their crime scene photographer and he knows lots of people on the street in Berlin. He's actually American, a Vietnam vet who stayed in Germany after he got discharged from the American hospital and married a German. Quill knows everyone on both sides of the law. I guarantee he can tell you the pimp's name and more, I'm sure. Get one of the Guardia men who can speak German or English well enough to make a conference call with you or something, because I know Quill can't speak Spanish."

Ballero took the paper and looked at me quizzically. "You have any more surprises in mind for me, Epiphany?" I immediately noticed he'd switched over to my first name, dropped the formalities he'd been using earlier.

I smiled and shook my head, "I hope not. These last two days haven't been much fun for me. My husband isn't so pleased with me either."

The older man smiled knowingly, and stood up, indicating our interview was finished. "I do understand, and I do appreciate how helpful you have been to us. I have to go quickly and join my men, but can you please meet Dr. Nunez at the ferry tonight and accompany him back to the morgue again for the autopsy?"

Did I imagine he hesitated before the next sentence?

"He specifically requested your presence."

I tried to hide my pleasure. "I have to go immediately to the German trekking station to get my weather data. I need it for both murders now," I explained, glancing up at the large round clock on the wall behind him. "But there's still plenty of time before the evening boat is due, and of course, I'm happy to help in any way I can."

I was kind of relieved that he didn't invite me along to the recovery scene.

Recovery from an aluminum boat surrounded by water isn't as complicated from an entomological point of view as a terrestrial recovery. The only thing the blood-spattered dinghy could tell me was that sun reflecting off metal surfaces would increase the rate of corpse decay. The development of eggs and maggots in Strawberry's throat, and eye sockets would have been accelerated by that heat.

For a brief moment, I imagined Ballero and his team boarding the police boat at the docks, motoring out to where I'd found her sprawled and abandoned like a Raggedy Ann doll with her eye buttons torn off.

The big man and I shook hands goodbye and I was hoping that with all I had to do before meeting Nunez, there'd be enough time in there for me to freshen up.

I could tell by the way the policeman was looking at my bedraggled hair and damp clothes sticking to me that I wasn't a very presentable sight.

13

At the open-air phone stand across from the *Habibe*, I dialed up Quill's mobile in Berlin. He answered eventually. His greeting was as usual minimalist: "Yep."

"It's me," I said, "calling you from Spain on a pay phone. Can you write down this number and call me back because I don't have enough change or a phone card, and I'm in big trouble."

"Wait a sec. I'm on my bike going to work."

There was a brief pause, "Okay, shoot."

I read out the number of the pay phone twice. We hung up and I waited for the phone to ring, looking about me nervously, but no one was nearby to overhear the conversation. I cursed myself for stubbornly refusing to get a cell phone like everyone else on the planet, but I always felt like it was being put on an electronic leash.

Both Mimmo and Quill were forever at me to get one. Quill and I had become friends before I'd met my husband because we are the only Americans on the same city league coed softball team. He's our star pitcher and I play catcher. He's an outstanding athlete, despite being over fifty *and* a pothead and beer drinker. He is a little slow running the bases, but he still got the MVP award at the end of our last season. The fact that he is so much older than me, and that he had three kids at home, all from different mothers who had run out on him, keeps our relationship strictly platonic, but there is chemistry between us nevertheless. I admire him. He is still handsome and tearing away at life with all his teeth. We work well together. Whatever the play, I always catch his throws and make the tag.

The phone rang. I put it to my ear. "Okay Stretch, this betta be entertainin', I'm standin' in a *Tabakladen* cuz it's rainin' cats and dawgs here." After nearly thirty years in Germany, he still had a strong Boston accent.

"You should expect a call from the chief of the local police in a short while. I gave him your extension, I figured you'd be on the night shift. His name's Ballero but..."

Quill interrupted me. "Are you in jail there or what?"

"Noooo, I haven't done anything, but I accidentally discovered a couple of dead bodies, two women that were murdered."

I was waiting for him to react but there was a loud silence on the other end.

To get to the heart of the matter I said quickly, "One of them was Strawberry Shortcake."

I thought I heard a sharp intake of breath. Quill knew the whole sordid story of Mimmo and Strawberry because I'd cried on his shoulder after finding out about it. He'd cooled me down and urged me to forgive Mimmo and forget about it.

"So here's the thing, I told this guy Ballero that I knew her and that she was a hooker from Berlin, but I never mentioned her connection to Mimmo or the restaurant because Mimmo is already pissed at me because I've been helping the cops on the first murder because it was clear to me that the body was *dumped* on the beach where I found it."

He interrupted me again, "Don't tell me. Let me guess. You were picking through maggots on the stiff."

"Well they weren't maggots exactly, but let me get to the point..."

"Hey, it's on my dime, Stretch, I want all the gory details."

"Quill, *listen* to me and stop asking questions because it's really serious. I worked the first autopsy with the pathologist here—they sent him in from Tenerife. Now he's asked for me to take part in the one tonight on Strawberry, and I have to meet him soon at the ferry, and I have to get to the weather station to get data and..."

"Okay! Cut to the chase, what do you need from me?"

"*Who's* that Russian pimp that's always with Strawberry at *La Strada*? Because I'm sure that's who killed her. He slashed her throat and left her in a dinghy on the ocean. Can you give his name to Ballero? I always kept way clear of them, so I have no idea ... I didn't even know her real name, we found that out from the health club, but I thought you might know something about that guy."

"Sure, I know. He's in the Russian mafia, sweetheart, and if I were you, I'd pack my bags and get on that ferry and come back to Berlin *asap*. Let those Spanish cops do their own dirty work. You don't want the Russian mafia on your tail!"

"Russian mafia? You sure about that, Quill, really?"

"I hope you don't look as wide-eyed as you sound, baby. His name's Mikail Petrov, but he's known around here as 'The Finger' because he's the third top-dog of the Tambovskaya-Malyshevkaya gang and he has his finger in everything in Germany. Money laundering, racketeering, drug dealing, prostitution, *and* the restaurant and hotel business, I might add. They say he's even had influence over banking institutions."

I noticed that I was shivering, and it wasn't just my damp clothes.

"Oh my sweet Jesus," was all I managed to reply.

"I'm not joking, Epiphany. *Get out of there* and tell Mimmo what's gone down, so he has a heads up while you're traveling and once you're back in Berlin. These people are the scum of the earth, and personally, I don't know why he ever let any of 'em in his place. I told him once when we were having a beer togetha that he was a crazy mothafucka to get within ten feet of that guy."

"Why didn't you tell me this before?" I demanded.

"Because you were so stressed out about him and that red-haired doll, and anyway, what exactly did you imagine that her boyfriend was, a dancer from the Bolshoi Ballet?"

"You gotta tell Ballero all this, but don't... *promise me...* you won't mention Mimmo or the restaurant."

"The team started spring practice last week, Stretch, get your ass back here."

"Promise me."

95

"Relax kid, your secrets are safe with me."

"Quill?"

"Yes darlin'." "What do you think they were doing here on La Sirena ... why here?" Silence—a dead pause. I thought we might have been disconnected.

Then I heard Quill talking in German to someone and I realized he was paying for his tobacco. He turned his attention back to me. "I dunno. Could be they were at a family reunion. The other two dons of the 'Troika' have their Bentleys and Ferraris parked in Spain now, I think Malaga, cuz the weatha is betta. Get out of there, Stretch."

Then the line really went dead.

I hung up the receiver and felt a panic rising from the pit of my stomach. I tried to recall the fortitude and resolve I'd felt while swimming back to shore. Anyway, it was way too late to change my mind. I was officially entangled in the first murder and was expected at the second autopsy in a little over an hour. *And* I had lied through omission to the police to protect my husband who was already angry with me *and* he didn't even know the half of it.

I was in deep.

14

Nunez and his assistant stood on one side of the table and the morgue diener and I stood on the other side, with the blue plastic body bag lying between us. The atmosphere was solemn, mindful of the dignity of the victim. I'd stopped calling her anything but Dora Hoch in my mind. She deserved at least that.

The diener unzipped the bag. Almost immediately the sickly sweet odor of rotting roses hit the cold air of the room. Nunez passed me a small bottle of oil and suggested I rub some on the inside of my mask. It smelled like wintergreen and blocked the stench of decay.

She looked terrible.

For a moment, we all froze at the sight of her, her marble white skin and dress soaked in blood, her eye sockets and gaping throat wound alive with maggots. The sharp talons of the birds that had feasted on her beautiful eyes had left reddened welts and scratches on her chin and the sides of her face. Her lips were slightly open, puffed and blackened by the sun. Her hair hung in seaweed strands, sealed by crusted blood in strange configurations on her breasts, on either side of her deep cleavage.

"She's wearing exactly what I saw her in last night at the Mirador," I said in a clumsy attempt to normalize the disturbing moment. I glanced down at her legs and realized the white leather Roman sandals were miraculously unscathed, considering the river of blood that had followed the severing of her carotid artery. Her dainty orange toenails still winked with diamonds.

I'd told Nunez as much as I could in our taxi ride up to the hospital. I felt comfortable with him, like we were old friends, but I had to withhold the full extent of my personal involvement with Dora. I only told him what I'd reported to Ballero and nothing more.

Nunez looked down at her impassively with complete focus, his eyebrows knitted together in concentration. The diener and the assistant lifted her legs while Nunez and I pulled the empty bag out from under them. They hoisted her upper torso while we slipped the bag off the table and over on to the counter— where I could check it for maggots that might have fallen off from the mass on her throat, or maybe even pupa that could have migrated from the body, or for adult flies possibly trapped inside at the time of the recovery.

I found several maggots and one small fly stuck in the seam of the lining. After putting them in separate vials labeled with Dora's name, the time, the date, and 'body bag', I turned back to the autopsy table to begin the job of collecting the remaining organisms and storing them for categorization and preservation. But before removing any of the maggots, I first had to measure the temperature of the heat generated by the feeding of the maggot mass. This would come into play later, when I computed all the other microclimate data into the equation that would help us refine our time of death estimation.

While a body on or near an aquatic environment normally decays at a slower rate due to a cooling effect, the opposite was true in Dora's case. Even though the day started out hot and humid, clouds had rolled in accompanied by a light wind. The aluminum hull of the dinghy had reflected the morning sun, slowly heating her corpse as if she had been in a cooking pot. The ocean breezes had carried enticing plumes to all the flies that were regular visitors at the garbage bins on the pier. The bacteria they carried and introduced into her wounds further accelerated the decomposition process.

"They've done quite a piece of work here to the neck wound, feasting on the open tissue. I don't imagine there will be any original edges to tell you what kind of knife was used. There was a hell of a lot of infestation and the maggot mass is pretty dense. I'm making a guess that they began arriving shortly after sunup."

When I finished my painstaking collecting, Nunez's assistant began cutting the cashmere dress off Dora's blood-encrusted torso, then her thong underpants, her jewelry, and her sandals were removed. She looked even smaller than I remembered.

If you didn't look at her demolished head, she was still an object of perfect proportions.

Nunez lifted her little wrist almost tenderly, removing the paper hand bags to look closely at her fingers and nails.

"No signs of a struggle. No defense." *Déjà vu for both of us.* Nunez's assistant began taking scrapings from under her nails.

I guessed at what Nunez might be thinking, but I waited for him to speak his mind when he was ready.

His fingertips gently moved over the soles of her feet, her ankles, her knees, her thighs. He walked around the table never taking his eyes off her, while speaking into a handheld tape recorder. "No visible *antemortum* injuries."

When he looked closer at the half moon cavern under Dora's chin, he noted what we already knew from the amount of blood sprayed all over the inside of the dingy. "Cartoid artery completely severed, partial decapitation." Then pushing back her left earlobe with his thumb, he continued, "Assailant right-handed."

I saw in my mind's eye Dora leaning back against the Russian, maybe looking up at the stars. He wraps his left arm around her locking her in place, then, before she can blink, he's placed the knife tip under her left ear, slices back to the right one, like gutting a fish.

"How did he get out of the dinghy?" I wondered out loud, spontaneously. "When I found it, there was nothing around, it was just drifting." Nunez shut off his recorder. "Oh, I'm sorry, it just occurred to me, I didn't mean to disturb you."

Nunez shook his head, *"No problemo.* I imagine he just jumped out and swam to shore, dropping the weapon in the water. The Guardia found nothing in the boat other than the victim. But my question would be why did the killer not dump her body overboard and just *row* away?"

I thought about it a moment.

"Maybe, someone picked him up in another craft, an accomplice," I suggested, thinking of my phone call with Quill ... *a family reunion.* "But I imagine he would've been covered in some way with her blood, and possibly he didn't want to risk the chance of being seen by anyone in the bloody boat ... in his bloody clothes. It would be better to jump in the water, strip and swim to shore somewhere. Even under cover of night, it seems it would be far riskier to stay in the boat."

"But why not dump the corpse as well?" interjected the assistant, momentarily distracted from his task at hand by our conversation.

Nunez answered quickly, "Bodies don't just conveniently sink to the ocean floor, Eduardo, you should know that by now! It would have washed into the shore sooner. The killer was counting on having some time to get away before anyone searched for him, I would guess. Bad luck for him that Epiphany was swimming around way out there, and that the wind today kept the boat drifting *toward* the coast and not further out to sea."

I thought about Ballero and wondered if he was making any headway on tracking down the Russian. I seriously doubted that The Finger would have travelled to La Sirena with his own passport, if killing his mistress had been on his vacation agenda. I thought about Dora sitting alone at the bar in the Mirador, and guessed the bartender would be the first witness Ballero interviewed. I glanced at the morgue clock and was startled to see how late it was.

I settled into a corner of the lab with my microscope to work on my specimens and take notes while Nunez continued the autopsy. I was dead tired but stimulated from being in Nunez's presence if not a little giddy from the alcohol fumes coming from where my maggots lay immersed in a watch glass, after being popped into boiling water to kill them. The heat from the water rapidly coagulates their internal tissues, keeping them fully expanded. This allowed me to estimate their age by the appearance of their spiracles, tiny openings on their thorax used for gas exchange.

I couldn't help but wonder if all this work Nunez and I were doing would ever count for anything. It seemed to me that a thug as famous and as powerful as The Finger would never be touched by the Spanish police, would never sit in a court of law and be brought to justice like an ordinary man.

It was a really depressing thought.

I was light-headed and hungry from not eating since morning. I was cold and uncomfortable in my salt-dried skin. I was worried about my husband who was waiting at home or more likely in a bar, wondering where the hell I was.

My neck hurt from being bent over the oculars of my scope for so long. I tried to stay focused on what I was doing, poking with tweezers at the ugly little creatures, measuring, making notations, keeping alert and accurate. In the background I could hear the noise of the autopsy proceeding behind me: the sounds of Nunez and his assistant moving around, talking softly while they collected trace evidence, took x-rays, incised into the body and examined internal organs.

The hands on the clock face moved closer to midnight. I had to finish.

I wanted to just take a break and eat a sandwich or something, but I knew that was impossible. I was so strung out that if I stopped I might have just collapsed and not been able to complete my job without making errors. Whatever the odds against us, we had to give Ballero and the Guardia as much information as we could, as quickly as possible, and all the i's had to be dotted and the t's crossed, so our evidence could withstand the attack of clever defense lawyers in the future. *If it came to trial at all.*

I was checking my weather data and crunching numbers on my pocket calculator when Nunez suddenly appeared at my side. I looked up at him startled.

"Epiphany, if your theory on the boyfriend is correct, I may have just found his motive," he said wearily. "I'm sorry to say your little friend was three months pregnant."

15

I peeled off my clothes; they dropped in a heap at my feet. I wanted to make love desperately, to savor my luck to be living, to leave the taste of death behind. Mimmo was lying in bed, lit by the blue light of television. Mostly was curled asleep in an armchair in the corner of the room.

Mimmo wasn't as drunk as I'd expected. He didn't say anything though he was dying to know where I'd been all evening. It was a pact we had made with each other somewhere in the beginning of our relationship: no ropes around our necks. His eyes burned through me.

I had to wash off the lingering smell of the morgue first.

I went into the bathroom and turned on a very hot shower. I scrubbed myself all over with a gel that smelled like oranges. I washed my hair vigorously, twice, with shampoo and then combed through it with a coconut cream rinse.

As I was wrapping a towel around me, my husband came into the bathroom. It started there, moved through the hallway and ended on the floor of the bedroom. It was what Amy dramatically calls 'blood on the wall' sex. More to the point, it was like a California firestorm driven by the hot Santa Ana winds ... dying down in brief intervals, only to explode again in a different location with renewed intensity.

Afterward we lay awake for a long time. Neither of us spoke.

Eventually, I began to cry. I told him where I'd been and everything that had happened since I found Dora's body in the boat. I explained that whoever Dora was, whatever she'd done in her life, I felt she deserved to be taken seriously and defended in death. I also explained that if I hadn't alerted Ballero as I did, I feared he and the Guardia would have confused the coincidence of the two murders and gone looking for a single madman instead of pursuing each case separately, following the trail and logic of the evidence.

Mimmo listened patiently and then covered his face with his big hands muttering complaining words in Italian. I knew from past experience that the best way to calm him down was to get him in the kitchen, and in any case, I was starving. "I haven't eaten since I was in Fellini's, and as you know that was not very much. I can't go to sleep like this."

Moving around a kitchen for my husband is like a meditation. Every move is graceful and precise. He's fully present in the moment no matter how trivial the task, which is why it distracts him. Unlike me, through sleight of hand he cleans *while* he cooks. In the end you sit down to a meal that looks like as if it had been arranged by an Ikebana flower master, and the kitchen is at peace as well.

While he was working, I sat at the counter where I normally sort my beetles and stroked Mostly, who'd woken up and come in to join us. Suddenly, I noticed three avocados next to a note on pink paper. Constanze Therese always included some avocados from her garden with the weekly supply of fresh linen sent down with her granddaughter. But this time there were no towels and sheets, just a note in Serenella's even and round handwriting: *"Funeral de mi madre es mañana mediodia. San Juan Bautista."* She was inviting us to her mother's funeral the next day at noon, at the church near the children's playground in the center of the town. I was touched that she wanted us there. I wondered if it would be appropriate to bring along Mostly, but if not I imagined I could leave him tied up in the shade somewhere outside the church.

No more Udo for babysitting, I thought, sighing.

I pointed to the pink paper.

"Did you read that?"

Not waiting for the reply I took an avocado, a basket of bread and a bottle of mineral water over to the table in front of the sliding glass door that led to our balcony. I opened the door despite the chilly night air.

We could hear the shrill, repetitive crying of the swifts roosting in the various crooks and crannies of the cliff that blocked the rising moon from our view. Only the lamps from the boatyard and the harbor bar reflected and twinkled on the sheltered bay. I lit a candle in the center of the table.

Mimmo put two small plates of *pasta al cecco* in front of us, and sat down at the table with Serenella's note in hand. We were looking into each other's eyes for the first time in what seemed like ages. He smiled ruefully.

"*Allora,* so now we go to Church and confess our sins."

"It's not going to hurt you to go to Mass for once, and to say a little prayer... at least for Serenella.

Besides, I'm kind of interested to see what it's going to be like. You know, who's going to be there..."

"Eh ... I can tell you what it's going to be like. It's going to be really sad and depressive, with Constanze Therese leaning on that little girl, crying and crying." Mimmo made one of those Italian body language punctuations, jerking his head to one side.

"What could be more tragic than that?"

"She *asked* us to come Mimmo. We have to be there."

"I know, I know," he agreed, reaching for the bread. "But Wednesday I go to get new tickets back to Berlin. You've done everything you can do here and I am seriously worried that Mikail Petrov—if he did kill that poor girl—is going to find out you are helping the police!"

"But what is the logic in that?" I cried, losing my fleeting composure. *"The guy lives in Berlin,* not on this silly island! If he wants to kill me he can just find me at *La Strada!* And why the hell did you ever let him through your doors in the first place? You must have known who he was?"

Mimmo got up from the table and walked over to the kitchen. He returned with a bottle of red wine and two more glasses.

"By the way, did you know who he was before or after you went into the wine cellar with his, ahem, *girlfriend?"*

"This was a long time ago Epiphany, I barely knew you."

"That's not the point! The point is that you brought this person ... this *mess* into our lives, and now you're acting like I'm this crazy person who's endangering us because I'm so serious about my work ... because I believe in some old-fashioned concept of law and order ... of ... of ... commitment to ...", I searched around for the exact words, "justice... justice for someone."

"Aghhh," he waved his right hand dismissively over the breadbasket, "You are just *committed* to excitement, to playing Cowboys and Indians."

I didn't rise to the bait because I knew that I was ahead. I had scored and his barb was only in retaliation because he knew it as well.

"I have a question," I said to him, bringing him back into the tragedy of Dora Hoch. "Why is pregnancy the reason to murder her, like Nunez suggested?"

My husband groaned. "Epiphany, the girl was a prostitute. If she was already three months along with a baby then she had probably refused an abortion. What was Petrov going to do with a family of some other man's child? And she knew too much about his personal business. He wasn't going to let her go off on her own."

"But why kill her here?"

He shrugged. "Why not? In Berlin, he's the obvious suspect. If he came here on a false passport, like you said earlier and he has witnesses to lie for him in Berlin, or wherever you said the Troika is in Spain, then they *can't* connect him to her murder.

All of a sudden I felt so tired I thought I could fall off my chair. A half a glass of red wine had hit me like bullet. It was going to be just as I'd thought in the morgue, Putin-face was going to get away with it, and all my carefully preserved, measured and described maggots would mean nothing in the end.

I stabbed half-heartedly at an avocado slice in my salad.

Then I thought about Serenella bringing us the avocados and the note. I had to put Putin-face and Dora Hoch aside, I had to concentrate on helping Ballero find out what really happened to Serenella's mother. At least there might be some justice for someone.

"Please, let's not make a decision on the return tickets right away," I said. "Let's just get through tomorrow, through the funeral, okay?"

Maybe he was worn out from drinking with Enzo all evening and the emotional rollercoaster with me, but he didn't press me any further.

After dinner, I took his mobile to call Amy.

"Please be in your office Audrey Hepburn," I silently prayed.

After six rings she finally picked up, "Gardiner here," she said breathlessly, as if she'd just come in from running a marathon. I could imagine her leaning over her desk to reach for the phone: a damp T-shirt clinging to her bony shoulders; her stick-straight, strawberry-blonde hair pulled into a knot at the top of her head, like a samurai warrior; a light sheen of sweat highlighting the delicate bone structure of her lightly freckled skin.

"Catch your breath Honey," I said, "It's only costing me ten cents a minute."

"Hotdamn, Sophia Loren! I was worried when you didn't answer my email, everything okay?"

"Yeah, I'm sorry about that, I've just been going non-stop since the uh... incident. Was it something important?"

"Nah, I was just whining some more about the trial, wassup with you?"

I couldn't tell Amy about the new murder or anything I was going through, I was too tired and dispirited. I just needed her help in making sure what I told Ballero tomorrow morning would be as close to truth as I could ascertain.

"I was wondering if we could go over my figures, can you pull up the formula on your computer?"

"You bet," she responded eagerly. "Okay, while I'm doing that, tell me if you've had more contact with Antonio Banderas."

I laughed, "Well actually I'm working on a second autopsy now but I can't really talk about it."

"Oh, I see," she responded, "the Italian stallion is in the room with you."

"Amy, do you have your program open? Okay, here are my figures; plug them in, I'll wait, then tell me what you think. I want to make sure we're on the same page before I stick my neck out with Ballero."

Laurie Taylor

I gave her the numbers.

"By the way," I added. "He's already barking up the wrong tree."

Amy was fast and after a few minutes, she'd gone through my calculations twice.

I continued, "The way I see it—if the body was that clean, it clearly was transported in a plastic tarp, so that of course would have offset..."

"Right," she interrupted me. "But let's work backwards first. You found her at 7:00 am. Oldest eggs in her wounds were borderline first instar. So that would put us at around 16 hours since oviposition, considering the degree days." Amy was referring to how measurements are calculated with precise weather data.

I nodded my head, then realized Amy and I were not in the same room, so I verbally agreed, "Uh, huh."

"So Sophia what's your problem with setting the death at around 8:30 Saturday night?"

"I'm following you," I said into the phone.

"So counting backwards 16 hours from when you pulled out those eggs from her wound at 12:30 Sunday morning, you get around 8:30 pm Saturday night, isn't that right?"

"Well that's why I'm calling you, because it doesn't make sense to me and here's why... her little girl last saw her at 11:30 Saturday morning when she left the house. She was expected at her bar at around 3:00 in the afternoon and she never showed up. Her bartender tried calling her cell phone after an hour or so and left a message, but he wasn't worried about it. He told Ballero it had happened before, and then when she didn't show at all he figured it was some kind of emergency with the family. So he worked the night alone"

"So?" Amy asked.

"So it seems to me that she was probably dead by 3:00, because if she knew she was going to be late, she would have called at least when she was over an hour late."

108

"But you just said she'd done it before, been late before and not called..."

"Yeah, but I think it would be too much of a coincidence that she just happened to be late, didn't call, and that then *much later* she was waylaid by her assailant and murdered. Occam's Razor tells us she was late because she wasn't coming *at all*, she was already dead!"

"If that's the case, her body was somewhere cooler and protected from insects for several hours, then placed outdoors in the late afternoon sun where it heated up enough to attract the first fly around 7:30 in the evening before it was dark, and then eventually transported after 3:00 in the morning when it could be brought down to the beach without anyone seeing."

"Uh-uh," I grunted.

"Now what's the matter with that scenario?" I could tell she was disappointed that I didn't jump on the bandwagon with her.

"Just that it's only a scenario. I can't go to Ballero with a hypothetical scenario and insist he free an innocent man. They hadn't even heard of forensic entomology here before I arrived. I need a tight case."

"Who's the innocent man?"

"Oh, a friend of ours, and I don't know why they even picked him up. But you'd only have to meet him for ten minutes and you'd agree with me that he's totally wrong."

"You're not going to have a tight case whichever way you cut it, sweetheart. Maybe the body was never covered at all, but then it would have had more infestation if it had been killed early Saturday afternoon. The eggs would be farther along... unless it was in someone's house or something, which is highly unlikely..."

I didn't say anything.

"*If* it was wrapped up ... but how could it have been wrapped up with a knife still stuck in the back? That doesn't make sense either, well I guess you could do it..." Her voice trailed off. I waited. She came up with a question I'd been asking myself. "Why leave the knife in there in the first place?"

109

Now I jumped in, "Look, Amy, my problem is it's like a loop. I can't really assess an accurate PMI without knowing *where* the body has actually been. I can't find out where it all took place without establishing a travel time! I mean, oh God, I don't know..."

My thinking was drifting off with my words. "Let me chew on it," she suggested brightly. "Yeah, good, just don't choke on it."

"Welcome to police work, Epiphany."

"Yeah, right, *mañana*."

I hung up the phone feeling worse than before I called. I felt like Amy wasn't taking me seriously. Maybe I hadn't felt able to speak clearly enough, to elucidate all the conflicting angles that made me so unsure.

I looked over toward my husband who was watching me from the kitchen. He threw back his head, tossing a lock of glossy dark hair away from his face, his warm brown eyes staring intently at me trying to judge my state of mind. Mostly wagged his tail, jubilant that I was now rightly paying attention to my family and no longer talking to a telephone. I was loved. I might be lacking in confidence, but I was not lacking in love. It made me feel a little bit better, able to go to sleep and hope that in the light of day something might be clearer.

16

The next morning, I was making breakfast, when there was an authoritative knocking on our door. Mimmo was out walking Mostly on the beach. I gathered my kimono tightly across my breasts and automatically opened the door without asking who was there.

Ballero's bulky figure filled the threshold, blocking out any daylight from the street behind him. Trying to hide my surprise and dismay, I invited him inside. He apologized for showing up so early, explaining that he needed to get the key for the Café Sport from my husband. I told him Mimmo was out for a walk with the dog, and I assumed Mimmo had put Udo's key on his own ring of keys, which he had with him, but I invited Ballero to wait and have some coffee with me.

While I made the espresso, he hung over my work counter under the kitchen window, focusing his attention on some shallow boxes of Carabidae beetles that I'd collected and identified over the past few weeks, before being drawn into the murders.

What never ceases to amaze me is the primitive revulsion for insects that apparently still lurks in the brain of a good proportion of the population. Even a macho like Ballero betrayed squeamishness when confronted with the fact that these six-legged creatures exist in abundance somewhere out of his sight, but not that far away from his jurisdiction.

The early morning eastern light coming in through the window accentuated the right side of his face. I noticed his skin was not only deeply lined from years of sun exposure, but he'd once had a problem with acne, which had left it pitted as well. *Rugose*, I found myself abstractly thinking in entomological descriptive terminology, as if his face were the pronotum of a beetle. I gathered myself together for the task on hand: to find out why he'd pounced so short-sightedly on poor Udo without any forensic evidence. But I had to do this in a way that wouldn't alienate him. I noticed he was picking up a box of *Brachinus* specimens.

"That species is really quite interesting," I remarked. "They're called Bombardier beetles because they have the charming habit of blowing a foul smelling, skin-irritating chemical gas out their ass when you disturb them, and it literally explodes, and makes a noise like this." I replicated the dry popping noise with a neat trick of my tongue and teeth. Amy and I used to practice this imitation when we came across them in the field.

Ballero cracked a smile exposing his badly nicotine-stained teeth. I went in for the kill.

"Would you like to drink your coffee with me on the balcony so we can smoke? I promised Constanze Therese we wouldn't smoke inside."

We stepped outside and sat down on the two molded plastic chairs. I was momentarily disconcerted to see my lacey underwear hanging on the drying rack in the corner. I put the coffees down on the table and went back inside for an ashtray.

Ballero offered me one of his unfiltered *Gauloises*, I accepted without hesitating. I'm not really a smoker except on the rare occasions when I'm drinking and so outnumbered by my husband and his smoking friends that I resort to it in self-defense. But I do know that accepting a cigarette from a smoker has a certain psychological bonding effect, even with strangers. I tried not to inhale too much as I hadn't even eaten breakfast.

"Are you going to search Udo's bar? Is that why you need the key?"

Ballero nodded non-committedly.

I thought I should subtly remind him that through my co-operation with Nunez, the Medical Examiner in Tenerife, I was still officially a part of the investigative team.

"I got confirmation last night on the egg evidence that we sent to the Madrid forensic laboratory on the age and species of the fly infestation. Also, Dr. Lopez and I identified the plant and insect evidence from her hair. Later this afternoon, we plan to go over his vegetation maps, but we're almost certain now that the killing must have taken place in an area on the south-eastern outskirts of the *Parque*, not far from..." I tried to think of a landmark that he would be familiar with in that area. I remembered the only paved road cutting through there eventually went by the Cueva Pintada, a historic site of aboriginal cave paintings.

"Somewhere near the Cueva Pintada," I added. Ballero raised one of his shaggy eyebrows in interest. "So, shortly we should be able to very precisely pinpoint the time of death." I said this with more confidence than I actually felt.

"Maybe Udo will have a confirmed alibi; maybe even he was seen in his bar at that time. What has happened to bring him under your suspicion?" I attempted to sound as polite and nonpartisan as I could.

"The murder weapon belonged to him," Ballero squinted against the sun and exhaled smoke as he spoke.

"There were no fingerprints Dr. Nunez told me."

"The weapon is a Tuareg dagger and he bought it at that African shop."

This new piece of information astonished me. Out of Africa was a shop located in the same alley as Fellini's. It was also run by one of the Italian gang: Gaetano, a skinny ex-bicycle racer with missing teeth who now sold imports from Africa. Sometimes he traveled there himself for the goods. I didn't know him well, but had looked around inside his shop. He never seemed to be doing much business. On occasion, I spotted him sitting in the cool, dark interior of the shop playing chess with a friend or customer, listening to African music.

I remembered that Nunez had remarked on the strangeness of the knife, how there was a pattern of scores that ran the length of the narrow and slightly curved blade. The handle had been made of three metals: brass, copper, and a white metal, fashioned together in a form that created a beautiful handgrip. I imagined Gaetano on his bicycle somewhere in the Saharan desert cutting a deal with an indigo-swathed Tuareg aloft a camel.

"So it's one of a kind," I said. "No question about it?"

"There were three of them. The Italian had three of them in his shop. He still has one; and he sold one to the German and one to an old Englishman, a tourist, maybe three months ago when he first returned from Mali."

"And why would 'the German' *want* to kill Esmeralda?" I asked as if I believed it was even in the realm of possibility.

Ballero hesitated for a moment. I was suddenly aware of how warm it was on the balcony, that the sky was absolutely cloudless, the air still, the ocean below sparkling but listless. It was going to be very hot at the funeral service inside that church.

"What motive could Udo possibly have?" I prodded.

Ballero spoke slowly and deliberately as though he were only developing his train of thought as he was speaking.

"He was very angry at Esmeralda and Constanze because they never told him about the harbor rebuilding before he signed the lease on his bar. He was losing money every month because of all the noise and dirt. The tourists were going to other beaches, and *then* when Esmeralda opened her disco in the evenings, that took away some of his night business as well."

"Well, there you go, Chief Inspector. If there were bad feelings between them, why in hell would she go for a long walk up in the mountains with him? Turn her back on him so he could swiftly stab her? Remember there were no signs of a struggle ... and, then, drag her body back and dump it onto the beach right in front of their businesses! That just makes no sense to me."

Ballero offered no defense of his theory. His gaze penetrated me. He seemed to be saying, *This is my island, you might know about bugs, but you know nothing about the people who live here and why they do what they do, so show a little respect!*

"Did you meet with Nunez this morning?"

Ballero nodded, "He told me the poor German girl was pregnant and the killer must have been someone she knew and trusted. It seems you might be right about the boyfriend, but there is no trace of the Russian anywhere. My men have asked everywhere, no Russian passports registered on the ferry line, at the hotel or at any pensions, so far."

"But certainly somebody must have noticed them somewhere, she was a real knockout. Every man who saw her would have remembered her!"

"Claro, but their eyes were all on her. We got only one vague description of the man she was with, and only that from a taxi driver who took them up to the Mirador, waited for them, and then drove them back to the harbor."

"But what about the dinghy? Did someone rent it to him or did he just take it?"

"He just took it. The owner is a fisherman who lives in Playa Miranda and he knew nothing about it at all."

"Nunez must have told you that the wound on the German girl was so altered by the maggots that he couldn't make any conclusion about the weapon?" The policeman nodded. "So in that case," I continued, "I assume you're treating it as an entirely separate killing? I don't know if you had a chance yet to read the report I left with Nunez, but all the entomological evidence tells us Dora Hoch was dead by 21:30 that evening, which means only an hour later after she was last seen by me and the bartender."

"By the taxi driver who left them at the harbor," Ballero corrected me.

"So in that case," I persisted, "since you have imprisoned one man for the first murder, this was clearly a different killer, unless by chance you have the wrong man in jail. If that is the case, there is still the possibility of a double murder by one killer, who clearly cannot be the owner of the Sport."

At that moment we both averted our gaze away from each other and down to the beach, where at the very far end, Mimmo and Mostly were rounding the cliff and coming back into sight. I felt a profound sense of relief. Standing up, I put my index finger and my thumb in my mouth and whistled so loudly that Ballero visibly started out of his plastic chair.

Mostly, who'd been trained from a puppy to come running at that call, jumped in the air, reversed his direction below the tide line, and came cantering towards our building, his hind legs kicking up a spray of wet sand behind him. Mimmo waved but refused to change his pace to keep up with Mostly.

Ballero smiled again. A man who appreciates my dog cannot be all that bad.

"Look Chief Inspector, just keep an open mind about Udo until we can really total up the scientific evidence. You know the Law requires criminal cases to be proved beyond a reasonable doubt. For a forensic scientist, it's our job to evaluate if the evidence supports the probability that the proposed scenario is true... not the probability of the proposed scenario being true, *if* I find certain evidence."

Ballero lit another cigarette and seemed to consider what I was saying.

"If you as a policeman ask me, 'How likely is it that the knife's owner is the murderer?' my answer would have to be that it is likely. But, on the other hand, if you had been evaluating a number of suspects, and you asked me, 'How important is the presence of the knife in evaluating each person's guilt?' I could assess a range of probabilities. The first question would only allow me to consider one possible answer. I can't say the person in question could *not* have been the murderer, but I can't go any farther than that. The second question allows me to consider which one of the possibilities is most likely." Ballero remained silent.

"After the funeral service this afternoon, I'm meeting with Dr. Lopez. Can you and I meet again later? I should make it back down from the *Parque* around seven tonight."

I felt I'd made some impact. He stubbed out his cigarette and rose to go, presumably to meet Mimmo down on the beach to collect the key.

"Thank you for the coffee," he said brusquely. "I'll be at the bar at seven o'clock," he pointed down to the Once a Day which was in clear view of our balcony. "I'll be waiting for you."

17

I couldn't breathe inside the church. It was packed full, people standing at the back and in the side aisles. The older women fanned themselves constantly, while frankincense and men's aftershave scents wafted around us. A carpet of flowers and candles layered the dais stairs leading up to the altar, compounding the choking sweetness of the limited air supply.

We'd arrived early because I wanted to be sure of getting a seat on the center aisle to get a better view of the congregation, and so that Serenella would know that we'd come to be there with her.

Mostly had been consigned to the care of some children waiting for their parents outside in the playground. We tied him under the shade of a jacaranda tree with a bowl of water. He was so pleased to be the center of attention, his belly being gently rubbed by two little girls, that he didn't protest when we left him.

There was a palpable tension that seemed to grow as we waited for the family's arrival and the beginning of the Mass. The organist, hidden from our view, practiced some chords, adding to the suspense. I wished I'd brought a bottle of mineral water with us. Mimmo sat stiffly next to me, looking exactly as he must have as a small boy on Sundays in his Italian hill town, dispirited and dreading the long day: church, dress clothes and shoes, the big boring dinner with the extended family.

My attention wandered to the saints above us. They stood within their own cupolas, on either side of the tall stained glass windows. I could identify most of them: Saint Anthony of Padua, Saint Francis of Assisi, Saint Theresa the Little Rose, their signature iconography unchanged through the centuries, their depiction interpreted by different artists, yet always recognizable. This particular collection of statues, carefully painted and richly clothed, was remarkable for the delicate, expressive faces. They all wore a hard-won peace, as though they too had suffered from inner conflicts and human indiscretions.

Once a Catholic, always a Catholic, I thought. Mimmo and I were typical cases: he sitting there begrudging and defiant while I was pining for a certainty and a faith that had slipped away.

The processional march began, and a woman's soprano voice filled the cramped church with the "Ave Maria." I turned around and saw two altar boys and a priest walking up the center aisle. Behind them, six men carried Esmeralda on a bier fashioned from thick grape vines, twisted and knotted to form a frame, in which her shiny lacquered white coffin rested. Though the vines were real, clusters of plastic purple grapes were hung from each end.

It was this absurd touch that undid me. Tears welled up in my eyes.

I wiped them away just in time to see Ballero, clearly taller than the other pallbearers, holding up the rear end of the bier, just a few steps ahead of Constanze Therese. Her head was bowed under a black lace mantilla, her left arm locked into the right arm of her granddaughter. She walked slowly, a shattered woman dragging herself into public view. Serenella looked straight ahead, her eyes ringed in dark shadows. She wore a simple navy-blue sleeveless shift, her hair pulled away from her face in a French braid, exposing tiny gold loops in her earlobes. A single white rose dangled from her left hand.

I recognized four other pallbearers: two were the men I'd first seen playing chess on Constanze's patio the day we arrived. A third was an older man I frequently saw in the grocery store in our neighborhood, and the fourth was Esmeralda's bouncer at the disco. They all wore suits and ties. The sixth man, heavy-set, with a thick gold chain around his neck was unfamiliar to me. When they finally reached the dais, they gently laid the bier above the flowers, stepped down from the stairs and took seats on folding chairs on the side. Serenella and Constanze genuflected at the altar before stepping into the first pew. Before following her grandmother, Serenella placed her rose on the bare lid of the coffin. Some woman wailed from the congregation.

Mimmo squeezed my hand.

For some reason, this was all more difficult than examining Esmeralda's cadaver had been. Then, I'd felt intellectually engaged, removed, like a journalist behind a camera covering a war. At this moment, Esmeralda's spirit seemed present, whereas on that steel table in the morgue she had been nowhere to be found.

So Ballero was a close family friend. This would explain among other things his eagerness to nab the killer despite conflicting evidence. I knew coming to the funeral would bring some insights that I needed.

But who was the man with the gold chain? He looked too young to be in Constanze's generation, but too old to have been of interest to Esmeralda. Did they only ask the bouncer because they needed a sixth man, or was he also in the inner circle of the family? I could put Mimmo on him to find out more.

I got a better look during the Communion when the congregation slowly filed up the center aisle and back down on the side aisles to their seats.

I recognized around me many faces from my daily life in the village. Most were islanders, but I saw a few of the seasonal tourists as well, including some of the Italians from the Fellini crowd. The manicurist Maria sat in a side aisle, hanging on to a slightly rounder, older version of herself, who must have been her sister. I thought about our conversation. What was the basis for the revelation that Esmeralda had said, so close to her death, that she'd become like her mother? Were some of the same people who tried to stop her from opening her club here today out of curiosity? Or maybe they were here to spite Constanze Therese, who apparently had made her own enemies with her unconventional behavior and what some people regarded as naked greed.

The Mass droned on.

* * *

The burial took place in a cemetery on the edge of town in the same high elevation vicinity as the hospital and the headquarters of La Guardia. We had a rented car for the day, as I needed to meet later with Dr. Lopez at his office up in the *Parque*. After collecting Mostly, we took the car, grateful for the air-conditioning, followed the hearse and the slow funeral parade.

Due to the shortage of soil on the island, bodies were no longer consigned to the earth but stored in marble mausoleums encircling the original graveyard. Just like in Italy, tall evergreen cypresses had been planted on the perimeter of the walls, inspired by the sacred association of cypress trees with the Roman god of the underworld, Pluto. The cemetery was on a hill with two distinct levels and a rough pathway through shrubbery connected the upper and lower echelons. The higher level was closest to the car park and was the older section of the two, encompassing the oldest graves in the ground. This was where Esmeralda was to be placed in a crypt bought and reserved in her family's plot many years ago, probably by Constanze Therese's grandfather.

We stood in a ragtag semicircle of about fifty people around the open crypt. The grapevine bier rested on the ground. Tufts of purple alyssum sprung out from the cracks between the loosely fitted flagstones. Behind us, two spindly trees served as an *improviso* broom closet, with a push broom and a dustpan hanging from the two wires strung between.

In the crypts, the coffins were interred feet first, with the head of the coffin closest to the opening. A bronze plaque, engraved with the dead person's name and dates, sealed off the tomb. Between the plaque and the outer glass window was a space about the size of two shoeboxes in which the deceased's family could place objects for permanent decoration. Artificial flower arrangements and small portraits of Jesus in his crown of thorns were popular choices. I hoped that Esmeralda's mortal remains would be consigned to eternity without such dismal companions.

Mimmo and Mostly and I stood towards the back, watching the ceremony from a discrete distance. The crowd recited prayers while the priest consecrated the crypt with incense and sprinklings of holy water.

I kept thinking how awful it was that Constanze Therese had brought Serenella along on this final leg of the funeral. I felt she should have been spared the sight of her mother's body being interred in a wall of stone.

Serenella seemed to be looking away from the crypt and the bier, staring out in our direction. I noticed her gaze was fixed slightly to the left of us, at a grave behind us. I turned around slightly so I could see better what she was looking at.

A yellow and grey chickadee with a black-and-white striped head was repeatedly swooping down from a nearby tree branch and tapping with its beak on the glass window. After a few insistent raps, the bird returned to the tree for a brief rest, and then resumed its fruitless rounds all over again.

I wondered if the bird was being fooled by a reflection on the glass, but it soon shifted its attention to a neighboring grave at a different angle. I could find no logical explanation for this. It reminded me of how my grandmother told me, that in her part of Mexico people believe the souls of their loved ones visit them in the form of giant moths, beating their wings against the lighted windows of their houses at night.

18

I liked to think of Dr. Lopez and his brethren as modern-day keepers of the Ark. As the *Parque*'s only botanist, it was his job to oversee and protect an assemblage of species that had coexisted since the Pliocene and Miocene eras. Due to climate change over the ages, they now only exist in the Macronesian archipelagos and in a few patches in the Mediterranean basin. On the summits of La Sirena virgin groves can still be found.

Dr. Lopez's research involved something called genetic rescue, the study of how to keep the gene pool of threatened species strong. The heart of the biogenetic preserve was a zone of about 2,000 hectares into which entry was very restricted. Only Lopez and a few other scientists were permitted into this primeval realm of lush, lichen-layered trees, shrouded in mosses and mist. He described it to me in poetic Spanish as "where the whispering of water seeps from a stone of silence." Encircling and protecting the enchanted heart of the *laurasilva*, three more zones of progressive access eventually led to the more degraded periphery of the park. There, in two crowded offices in the back of the Visitors Center, Lopez and a graduate-student assistant maintained an archive of floral and faunal samples with accompanying files of electronic data.

Despite his slight, bent, and graying exterior, the elderly Dr. Lopez emanated unflagging energy. Over coffee and printouts of various database inquiries, GIS maps, species indexes, field notes and a grass sample, we discussed the probability of my finding a limited locale where the murder could have taken place.

"Of course, you couldn't have had better luck, that the poor girl's head rolled over a cricket that some bird had yet to snap up," he said wryly. "But then again, your bad luck is that we don't map to such a fine resolution with grasses that we can pinpoint exactly where you might find those species growing in proximity to *Laurus azorica*." He pointed to the lilac-colored polygons on the multi-colored vegetation map. "Those only represent grass types, not specific species."

I couldn't disguise my obvious disappointment.

"But then again, that's really not a problem, because when we granted those German girls permission to survey within the *Parque*, we had to go through a process which involves paperwork and the understanding that all field notes and voucher samples would be duplicated for our records as well."

Of course, I already knew this, as I too had to do the same in order to collect for the Berlin Museum. I forgave Dr. Lopez for this momentary lapse of his memory.

His slender, age-spotted fingers flicked through a set of index cards. I noticed he wore a gold wedding band on his left hand. I wondered how his wife could stand the endless work schedule he seemed to maintain at the *Parque*.

"This includes their collections outside the protected area. I can take you to the area where the *Sabulosa grillo* was collected and at least show you what those grasses look like, so you know what to look for."

I knew exactly what Lopez was getting at. My first botany professor had explained to me that recognizing plant species in the field was far easier than identifying them from dead samples carefully preserved in paper, or illustrated in a book. "Plants are like people," she'd said. "When you suddenly recognize someone you know in a crowd, you recognize them from a myriad of intangible sensory clues that are hot-wired to your unique experience of them."

It was true for plants as well. With them, it was subtle things like how their petioles or leaves moved in a breeze, or what other plants they kept company with.

"Then you're on your own," Lopez continued. "The good news is that *Laurus azorica* is not the dominant species in that general area, in fact it's quite unusual to find them in such an exposed situation."

If that was the good news, I was wondering what the bad news was.

"The bad news is those trees need a well-draining soil, while those grasses thrive in microclimates with more moisture pooling and condensation. So, while they both exist at the same altitude it's unlikely to find them side by side."

"But it *could* be possible?" My voice sounded whiny even to my own ears.

He tilted his head slightly, considering my question. "In the transition zones, where the remnant forests have been fragmented by roads, invasive species, and bordering agriculture plots... yes, a lot is *possible*. But it will take some hours of hiking around that terrain and getting a feel for it. You know what I mean?"

I knew exactly what he meant. This wasn't my first time in an unfamiliar habitat looking for rare species, or as in this case, a rare combination of two species in close proximity.

"And no getting distracted by beetles!" He admonished me good-naturedly.

"I'll try," I promised.

Dr. Lopez insisted that we take his truck, and not our rented car, so I politely acquiesced. As we climbed the road leading out of the basin of the park, he asked me more about the murder investigation.

"What are you hoping to find exactly if you *are* able to find this location?"

"I don't know, really," I answered. "But as we suspect the body must have been moved from the killing spot to a vehicle and then dumped on the beach." I rolled down the window on my side to get more sensory contact with the landscape we were moving through. "I imagine there's a good chance to come up with some sort of physical evidence. Even just finding the murder site, based on the odds of finding those trees and grasses together, will help me establish more exact climatic data on the eggs we found in the wound."

Lopez kept his eyes on the narrow winding road, furrowing his eyebrows in thought. "But just because those German students recorded that katydid species only in these grasses, it has not yet been established beyond a doubt that this is the *only* plant association on the island where the *grillo* can be found."

"No, of course not. But remember we're not trying to send someone to prison on the hair evidence... at this point we're only trying to get some understanding of how the wound could have been infested twice with so much time intervening, and maybe find some other evidence as to who was with her."

Lopez made a sharp turn off the paved road down a hairpin dirt track that curved back in the direction we were coming from. I momentarily stopped talking to take in the scenery, making mental notes so that I could find my way back here with my own vehicle the next day.

"The eggs were separated by 12 or 13 hours in development," I continued, "and that's one factor that tells us the body was moved. If I can synchronize the egg development under the appropriate microclimatic conditions with the travel time limits between the two locations, then, combined with the other information Ballero has—like the last time she was seen alive—we have a solid time of death."

"How many suspects are there?" asked Lopez.

"Just one as far as I know, and Ballero had him locked up."

"Why?"

"Because he had business problems with Esmeralda, and also because he once purchased a knife identical to the one that was taken from her body." At this point, I was tempted to bring up the second murder with him, but then I thought better of it.

"They already have the murder weapon?" Lopez sounded confused.

"Yeah," I admitted, "But no prints, and the knife was a Tuareg dagger, one of three sold by that African import store near the docks. Well, actually only two were sold, one to the German in jail and another to a British man some time ago, a tourist."

The old botanist looked over at me briefly, his eyes brightly amused. "And something tells me you don't agree with the police."

"I think Ballero is not experienced in murder cases. I think he is a friend of the family and I think there's a lot of social pressure on him to come up with a tidy solution that's not going to rock anyone's boat."

Lopez nodded his head. "An unsolved murder on the beach is not a tourist recommendation for the town."

I wanted to say, "Yeah, and with a second one following right on its heels it's gotta be a downright disaster!" But instead, I just added, "My thoughts exactly, and Udo—the guy they have in jail—is a foreigner. He's been here six years; he's single, in debt, not so well connected, and on his way to being an alcoholic. Kind of an easy target to quietly pin a murder on and bury in prison."

We pulled off the dirt road into a turnout. Lopez killed the engine. We got out of the truck and started down a steep trail. I kept talking.

"Look, Dr. Lopez, I don't at all mean to imply that Chief Inspector Ballero is crooked... or even incompetent for that matter. I just think it's hard for him to be objective. In our own field, sometimes the biggest discoveries were delayed—not because earlier scientists lacked the right technology—but because the prevailing social beliefs kept them from making the connections that later became obvious to someone who wasn't so blinkered."

"Claro," Lopez readily agreed with me, "Often, they could not even ask the right questions."

The rough path we were on, marked with mini-cairns, seemed to be descending into a gorge. As I'd come directly from the funeral, and hadn't even entertained the idea that Lopez would offer to personally show me the type of habitat I'd be looking for, my dress sandals were not up to the job. I had to concentrate more closely on where I was placing my feet.

Eventually, we came to a clearing, where to my surprise we found a small house with a corrugated iron roof, a green door, a dry-stone porch, and no windows. I immediately found myself thinking: *Isn't this is a good place to store a body until you can safely arrange it on the beach in the early hours of a Sunday morning?*

"Someone living here?" I asked Lopez.

He shook his head. "Not for many, many years. It's what the locals call a 'ghost house'. In some *barrancos* there are entire ghost villages that were abandoned after the German blockade in 1917. Export trade in the islands died out during that time, and many people from Sirena, as well as on the other islands, emigrated to Cuba and the Americas."

I took a closer look. Lopez followed behind. "There's a little outhouse in the back, and I think it still gets an occasional visitor, maybe a lost goat or someone hiking around up here looking for plants. I used it once myself."

Thankfully, I'd relieved myself at the Visitor Center, so I didn't feel the urgency to inspect the outhouse, but I did wonder if we could get inside the house. There was no lock or bolt on the front door.

Lopez turned away and headed back down the trail.

I checked my GPS watch. I would look around the house more carefully tomorrow when I was on my own. I didn't want to waste this kind man's time. Despite his advanced years, he was barreling ahead of me down the steep trail swinging his arms with gusto, as if he were using Nordic walking sticks.

I thought about the reality of getting a body back up this ravine. If we were remotely near the killing spot, it would have certainly taken two people to carry it in a tarp—or maybe on a sure-footed animal? Lopez had mentioned goats, but goats were probably too small to carry the deadweight of a woman who weighed at least 130 pounds.

19

Just as I'd done with Nunez, Ballero and I sat sheltered from eavesdropping at the corner table directly under the ceiling-suspended television. Above us, Real Madrid was losing to AC Milan, so we might as well have been invisible as well as inaudible to the rest of the Once a Day clientele. Ballero brought us two brandies from the bar and lit up a stinky cigar. I spread out the map Dr. Lopez had given me on the round Formica table.

"Here's where Dr. Lopez and I were." I pointed to a spot just north of Painted Cave. "I don't want to bore you with all the scientific details, but the end of the story is this: the earliest batch of eggs is around 12- 13 hours old. That type of fly doesn't fly or lay eggs at night. The body must reach a certain threshold in the decomposition process before the fly will be attracted to lay its eggs. How quickly the body decomposes and how quickly the eggs develop is affected by ambient climatic conditions. The *Parque* keeps weather data: hourly temperature, humidity, cloud cover, precipitation, wind speed and direction. For the purposes of his own research, Lopez keeps this data on the unprotected areas bordering the *Parque* as well, even at lower altitudes like in the *barranco* near Painted Cave. I also got similar data for the bay and the harbor beach from a private weather station at that German trekking place on the Punta. I also used it on the German girl's corpse."

Ballero was listening intently, but Udo might as well have been sitting right there at the table with us. The Chief Inspector and I both knew he didn't really want to understand what all this meant to his case.

"Those German grad students found those *grillos*... the same species we found caught in Esmeralda's hair band, they found them here," I tapped on the map with the unnatural, extended purple fingernail of my right index finger.

"Now, when I take all the climate data for both locations, the valley floor of the *barranco* and the harbor beach, and I apply it to what we know about corpse decomposition and fly life cycles, there is only one possible explanation."

I hesitated as I realized I had misspoken.

"Actually, there are two possibilities, and that is wherein our mystery lies."

Ballero's hazel eyes fixed on me with the intensity of a cat's sudden interest in the fluttering of a moth.

"We extracted the second batch of eggs from the stab wound at 12:30 during the autopsy, but as the body was in refrigeration in the morgue from around 8:00 in the morning, development would have stopped then, or at least slowed down considerably. In any case, they'd reached eclosion—which meant they were on the verge of becoming larvae, first instar maggots." At this point, the brandy-drinking, cigar-puffing Ballero astounded me by quoting Shakespeare: "We fat all creatures else to fat us, and we fat ourselves for maggots." And he raised his glass to me as if this were a toast.

Somewhat flustered by this new insight into Ballero's character, I attempted to carry on with a brief acknowledgment of his literary prowess. *"Bravo,* Hamlet!"

He smiled.

I continued with my explanation. "This is where we get the approximate figure of 16 hours. But that is an estimate depending on degree hours, that means 16 hours at a constant temperature of, let's say, 15° Celsius. We know at that stable temperature, this bluebottle fly takes a certain number of hours to grow from an egg into an adult fly, and in the first 16 of those hours it will only get from an egg to its first stage as a larvae. So if you count back 16 hours from when the body entered the morgue, 8:00 o'clock Sunday morning, you arrive at 4:00 o'clock Saturday afternoon. We know the body was not lying on the beach then —with no one noticing it—so we rule out the beach entirely as the murder scene."

Ballero looked as if he wanted to ask a question, but then he waved his cigar hand at me, indicating I should continue.

"While I haven't found the exact spot where the murder took place, as I have yet to find a *Laurus azorica* growing in the area around Painted Cave—that will take some hiking around up there—in all probability it's somewhere near there."

Ballero was really knocking back his drink.

"So when we apply the weather data for Saturday morning, afternoon, and evening, and presuming the body was exposed to some sun and not covered or in the shade, we come to the conclusion that death must have to have occurred earlier than 4 o'clock, because the corpse needed more time in the warmer hours of the day, when there was no cloud cover and no wind. But here's the mystery..."

I went to take another swig of my brandy and realized my glass was completely drained. Ballero smiled, formally excused himself, Spanish gentleman that he was, and went to the bar, returning minutes later with refills for both of us.

"So as I was saying, what's really interesting is how little infestation there was. It looks like one fly left her eggs deep under where the wound was not entirely plugged by the knife's hilt. Then, many hours later after it had been dumped on the beach, and the morning air reached the threshold temperature where the bluebottle becomes active again, another fly managed to lay more eggs on the surface of the wound before I trapped her. This suggests that when the earlier fly arrived, the body had only just reached the state of decomposition when flies are attracted, and then almost immediately the corpse was removed from the open air. Covering it wouldn't have been adequate. Once stimulated, these flies are persistent and find their way through almost anything."

Ballero nodded. I drank some more from my glass.

"So, the murder happens outdoors, earlier in the day when it's hot down there on the floor of the valley." I tapped again on the map. "Then the killer leaves the body alone for a while, but eventually decides to move it. It remains in a cooler spot protected from flies until it's safe to unload it on the beach."

Ballero cast his eyes back down onto the spot and wrinkled his forehead as though reading the map for directions. I saw a light go on in his head. "Can these flies get into the trunk of a vehicle?"

"Depends on the condition of the car," I answered. "A car in good condition, no rusted out spots near the trunk, probably not. But even if the car were parked in the shade, decomposition would have continued, just not at the same rate as outside. Faster, slower, depending on where the car was parked."

Suddenly, there was an outbreak of cheering and table thumping. Real Madrid had finally tied the game. We had to wait a minute until things quieted down before we could go on talking.

"What about the caves?" asked Ballero, once we could hear each other again. "Could they have hidden the body at Painted Cave?"

I scrunched up my face to indicate that while this wasn't a bad idea it wasn't a great one either.

"Well, you can get in there very easily from the road, but it would be risky, considering the caves are marked on most tourist maps and people actually go up there looking for them."

"Then what's your second possibility?"

This startled me as I'd momentarily forgotten that I'd introduced all this by saying there was more than one possibility.

"Esmeralda was killed even earlier in the day, say 12:30, inside a... house or hut, where it was cool and there were no flies. Then later in the day while it was still warm outside, her body was transferred. During the moving of the body, the back of the head came in contact with the forest floor and caught the stuff in her hair."

"And where were they moving it to?"

"To the car or truck or whatever it was they had parked out near the road."

"And the flies?"

"The wound attracted one fly—or maybe more than one—but from the amount of eggs I took out, I'd say only one was successful during the transfer of the corpse to the vehicle, and after that it was sealed off from any more flies."

"So we're looking for a building up there, a house in the forest near Painted Cave?" I wanted to go back alone. I didn't relish dragging Ballero and his men behind me while I looked for *Laurus azorica*, and I wanted to explore the inside of that odd little house by myself.

"Tomorrow morning, as soon as it gets light, I'll go back up there looking for the tree, or trees. I didn't have enough time today. If I find something, I'll call you and we can meet up on the Painted Cave road," I was quick to assure him.

Ballero nodded in acquiescence, blowing a cloud of smoke in my direction. I imagined he wasn't exactly keen on any unnecessary strenuous exercise. "You'll have to go to the *Parque*, and use Lopez's phone. There's no reception up there for mobile phones."

I thought I should mention the ghost house. "Lopez and I did see a little house up there not far from the valley floor where the *grillo* samples were collected." Then I quickly changed the subject. "What about Udo?" I asked. "Did he have an alibi for Saturday around noon?"

The Chief Inspector flicked his cigar ashes into the ceramic ashtray weighting down one corner of the map, and cleared his throat. "He wasn't seen in his bar until after four that day..." His sandpapery voice trailed off.

"So no alibi?" I hoped my disappointment wasn't that obvious.

"He said he was sleeping earlier in the morning... alone." He tacked on the qualification somewhat embarrassed. "He went to the Post Office at noon, before it closed for the weekend, to mail a birthday present to his mother in Germany. There was a long queue, so plenty of witnesses, *and* he had the receipt with the time stamped on it," Ballero admitted. He seemed to shrink into himself like a balloon progressively deflating.

The next thing I knew the bar erupted in pandemonium. Spain had won. Ballero sprung out of his seat and stepped backwards to get a look at the TV.

"The eleven-meter penalty goal!" He roared at me. I smiled broadly, more for Udo than for the Spanish football team.

20

Amy didn't answer her phone at home and she wasn't at her desk yet, although it was already 11:00 in the morning California time. I asked her colleague who finally picked up if she was at the courthouse as I remembered she was going through a trial, but he didn't think so.

"I'd try the boxing gym," he offered once I explained I was calling from Spain and that it was an urgent personal matter. "Do you have her cell number? I'm not allowed to give it out."

"Yeah, sure I do. I'll try it. Thanks." I was at a phone booth overlooking the boatyard and the harbor. I knew calling a cell in America was going to use the time on my phone card quickly, but I was eager to talk over the new developments with Amy. If she was actually fighting, I doubted she would answer her phone.

I was in luck.

"This better be good, Sophia Loren," she answered on the fourth ring laughing. "I was in the middle of my shower and I'm dripping wet with soap in my hair."

"How did you know it was me?"

"Just a good guess. What's happened?"

 "Well for one thing, I think I got the Get Out of Jail card for our friend Udo." "Really? That was quick!"

"I essentially used your theory that Esmeralda was killed much earlier in the day Saturday, but the body was stored somewhere, protected from heat and insects. But here's the twist ... we were always assuming that the stuff in her hair got there somehow while she was being killed, *outside* on the ground."

"Right..."

"But if she were killed inside a house around noon, and the body was moved later in the afternoon or early evening before it got dark, it could have been infested during transportation—which would explain why it seems only one fly managed to lay eggs."

"Bingo!" said Amy.

"That also might mean the head picked up the blossoms and the leg *after* death, while they were trying to move it. I was up there yesterday with the botanist from the park. He showed me where the *Sabulosa* was collected last summer. And there was this abandoned little house nearby with no windows, a terrace, and an outhouse. But it was quite a hike in there from the nearest place where you could park a car or a truck."

"No windows? Why have a house with no windows?"

"Lopez explained to me that it's an old style of building simple houses in the *barrancos*. I guess it was a practical design for the weather up there."

"But the tree with the flowers, did you find it as well?"

"Not right there, I need to go back up in the morning and explore the surrounding landscape a bit." "Are the police going with you?"

"No. I persuaded Ballero I would call him if I found the *Laurus* tree."

"What? What kind of policeman is he?"

I laughed. "Well, he had just downed a lot of brandy and he's kind of fat and out of condition, so I guess it didn't sound like such an appealing activity, unless he knew exactly where he was going and for what. But he did offer up that Udo had a tight alibi for midday Saturday."

Just then I heard the warning beep.

"Amy, I gotta talk fast, I only have two minutes left on this card. Here's my question for you. I'm emailing you my new calculations using the daily weather stats I got from Lopez that he keeps on that area where we think the murder took place. But here's my burning question. What the hell was Esmeralda doing way up there in the middle of the day, in the middle of nowhere? It's like an hour drive from town, and then another 30-minutes steep hike in there from the nearest road. If you're not a botanist, or an entomologist, or a *goat*, what could possibly make you go there?"

There was a moment's silence while Amy thought about my question.

Then she answered slowly, "A man I wanted to sleep with ... or ... someone who had something I needed very badly ... power, someone who had a hell of a lot of power over me and someone I didn't..."

And then the line went dead.

Being cut from the comfort of Amy's voice seemed to instantly extinguish the glowing feeling from the brandies and my success with Ballero. I was really hungry, tired, and my feet were aching from climbing around all afternoon in silly strap shoes. I thought about going to find Mimmo and Mostly, but I figured they'd be at Fellini's and I wasn't in the mood for socializing. So I decided to just go home, take a hot shower and eat whatever I could throw together quickly.

When I opened the door to the apartment, I was surprised to hear the television on in the bedroom, and it was odd that my dog wasn't coming to greet me. I entered the room cautiously and was astonished to see Serenella sitting on my bed with Mostly curled up in a ball in her lap. She was watching *Baywatch* dubbed in Spanish.

"Honey! What are you doing here? Where's Mimmo?"

"He asked me to babysit Mostly," she answered softly.

"Does your grandmother know you're here?" I realized by the timid expression on her face that she thought I was upset. I reached down and gave her a kiss on the cheek and a little hug. Mostly lifted his head up and kissed me too. We laughed.

"He told me Mostly can't stay alone in the apartment and he doesn't like the smoke in the bars," she explained, "My grandmother said it was fine. She had so many people at the house all afternoon, she said she needed some time by herself."

He doesn't like the smoke in the bars. That was a good one. I could see Mimmo was reaching out to Serenella in his own way.

"Hey, come in the kitchen with me, I think we have some ice cream in the freezer."

She followed me down the hall carrying Mostly like a bag of groceries with one arm. Her pink and silver phone, clipped on a long black ribbon repeatedly printed with the word 'Corona' in white letters, dangled from her neck.

I turned on the light in the kitchen. She sat down at the counter to look at my beetles while I served up the ice cream in dishes. Ice cream on an empty stomach and two brandies. I was going to be in trouble.

"On second thought, I'd better eat something healthy before I eat my ice cream."

"Didn't you eat dinner?" she asked me. I shook my head.

"Where were you?" I noticed she was looking closely at my feet. It occurred to me what an odd sight I was. I was still wearing my good black linen dress from the funeral, but my feet were filthy, my legs scratched and welting up from a reaction to some plant.

Just as I was debating exactly what to say to her, she had already dismissed the question and was on to something else. "What do you really *do* with all these bugs?" She gave a little wave with the free hand that wasn't keeping Mostly firmly on her lap.

"I'm taking them back to the Museum where I work. Have you ever been to a Museum of Natural History?"

"I've never been anywhere except Tenerife that I can remember, but I really want to go to California some day!"

I laughed, "Well I promise you it's not very much like *Baywatch*, but it has its good points." I put a tortilla on the electric burner to toast and grated some cheese on top of it. The ice cream was still sitting on the counter waiting to be consumed.

"But what do they want with all these bugs? Does it hurt them when you stick the pin in them?"

"No, they're already dead. I put them in the freezer to kill them quickly. They just go to sleep." As soon as the words were out of my mouth I wanted to take them back. I looked up from the stove and over to her. She had bent her head down against Mostly's head, her hair falling in a curtain over her face.

I walked over to them.

I put my hand on her neck. "I'm sorry, honey, I'm so sorry..." I could smell the tortilla burning. I gently ran my fingers through her straight silky hair, gathering it back behind her ears into a ponytail. A tear dripped off her chin on to Mostly's ear. Then her thin little shoulders began to shake, and she was quietly sobbing and Mostly started whimpering and anxiously licking her face.

"Here," I said, "Let's just turn off the stove so I don't burn the house down, and we'll all sit on the sofa together." I took her hand and pulled her off the barstool. She put down Mostly and we shuffled around the counter to the stove and I switched it off and turned the fan on to suck up the smoke. Serenella was crying louder now and choking a little on her mucus. I wiped her face with a tea towel and made her blow her nose before we went back over to the sofa.

As soon as we sat down, Mostly jumped up from the floor, wedging himself between us. She rested her head on my shoulder and gradually calmed down. The three of us sat like that for a long time. There was nothing to say.

* * *

After finishing the melted ice cream, I brought her home up the hill. There were no street lamps on the private road leading up to Constanze Therese's large house, but it was full moon and we could see our way without much trouble. Mostly was slow going up the stone stairs as they were too broad for him to take in one jumping stride. We passed the aviary, the parrots already asleep, hiding their heads under their wings. There were no lights shining from the house. I began to feel nervous.

"Constanze Therese," I called out in a loud voice as we walked across the terrace. Before I could stop her, Serenella used her key and darted into the dark house. She reappeared a few seconds later, after switching a light on in the kitchen. "She must be in the back garden."

A high wall enclosed the garden with a black wrought iron gate opening inward from the terrace. Serenella pushed on the gate and it swung open. In the wash of moonlight we could see a long table covered by a faded patterned oilcloth, surrounded by empty wicker chairs. I was about to turn back toward the house when I noticed a candle burning in a dim corner. A voice seemed to come from nowhere. "Baby girl? Is that you?"

I walked closer to the flickering candle and there in the shadows of a massive old avocado tree sat Serenella's grandmother, a gold rosary in her left hand and a glass tumbler in her right. A stub of a candle burned on an empty chair next to her. Melted wax was pooling up against an open bottle of Cinar and dripping down the chair leg. Constanze Therese was really drunk.

Serenella didn't seem to notice. She encircled her arms around her grandmother's neck and kissed her on the cheek. Constanze Therese tried to lift her arms to embrace her granddaughter but the tumbler in her unsteady hand was full and she appeared to be overwhelmed by the task.

"Go to bed, my sweet baby girl," she whispered. I saw in her body language that Serenella now grasped the situation. She came over and hugged me briefly, "Goodnight, Epiphany, see you tomorrow?"

"We'll see you at the beach in the afternoon, I promise." She bent down and kissed my dog between his ears, and returned to the house.

"Sit down, sit down!" Constanze Therese thrust her rosary-clutching hand out toward me and motioned to pull up a chair close to her.

The last thing I desired at that point in time was to sit down and have a conversation. All I wanted was a hot shower, a soothing cream on my legs and feet, and my bed. But the woman had just buried her murdered daughter that morning. So how could I refuse? I dragged over one of the wicker chairs.

"Have a drink! It's a fine Italian liqueur made of avocados." She handed me her glass and began drinking straight from the bottle.

"Artichokes," I politely corrected her. "Cinar is made from artichoke hearts." I pretended to take a sip.

She laughed. "Well that's right, if it was made from avocados, I'd be a rich woman!" She waved the rosary hand vaguely to indicate the big avocado tree behind her. This was something I'd heard before from wealthy people: 'I'd be rich...' as if they wanted to believe they were still in the middle class with the rest of us.

Damn, I said to myself, what's coming next? Is she going to vomit? Am I going to have to carry her into the house? What if Serenella finds her passed out here in the morning?

"Where's that handsome husband of yours?"

She leaned forward to look in my eyes. Maybe it was the effects of the moonlight, but for the first time I realized how Constanze was still really attractive for her age. She was wearing only a lace slip and a short, form-fitting crocheted sweater. A gold cross hanging on a chain nestled in her considerable décolleté, but she had on those ugly nylon knee socks so popular with older Spanish women. Her bare thighs still looked strong and shapely. The drink had brought a fire into her face. Her dark eyes under penciled brows were sad, but proud and seductive.

"I'm ... not sure," I stammered, afraid of where this was leading. "You give him too much freedom, that's a mistake with a man like that."

I was too startled to respond.

"I always see him alone on the beach and in Esmeralda's bar!"

She said her daughter's name as if she were still alive.

"Why do you spend so much time by yourself, jogging around up there in the mountains?"

"I like it," I protested, "It's my passion, really, nature, being alone in nature and trying to understand how everything fits together."

"Passion? There's only one passion."

In my mind's eye, I saw again those pictures of Christ suffering with his crown of thorns, propped up with the plastic flowers in the windows of the tombs. Oh, no. She's going to tell me the only passion is for God, the passion of Christ. But she surprised me.

"The only real passion is what can happen between a man and a woman." I took a gulp of the Cinar. "Passion is *losing* your mind, not using it," she continued. I looked around to see if she had any cigarettes lying about.

She was oblivious to my agitation.

"The only thing that saved me was my Papa left *everything* to me. Money saves a woman from the needs of her own body ... without money a woman is a *slave*, a slave to a man and to her whole family," she spat out.

As uncomfortable as I was, I knew this was as good a time as any to get some questions answered.

"But what about your sister? If you got everything, what happened to her?"

She apparently had no curiosity as to how I knew she had a sister.

"She had to marry the first man who asked her." She said this simply, as if it were a rule of law. "But God blessed her with a good man... Diego is a decent man, not a handsome man, but a good man."

She settled back into her chair and drank from the bottle again. Then the tears began and her voice was almost inaudible. I had to strain to understand what she was saying, "Esmeralda was his niece. We didn't see them so often. My sister and I have had our differences with each other. God knows I haven't been such a good person, but dear sweet Jesus, my daughter, my only child... like this ... to take her like this..." Constanze Therese was drifting in her pain, in her private sea of remorse and shock.

There was a dry rustling in the bushes near us. I started out of my chair, and then realized it was only Mostly chasing after something alive under a thick pile of fallen leaves. Just as I sat back down, I heard the scraping of the iron against stone behind me. I jumped up again and looked behind to see Ballero's substantial form squeezing through the narrow gate.

Diego Ballero. It all made more sense. Ballero wasn't just a friend of the family, *he was married to the disinherited sister*. That's why he'd been one of the pallbearers. That's why he was blindly rushing to justice. Why hadn't anyone ever mentioned this to me at Fellini's? They probably assumed Mimmo and I knew it already. I remembered Pepe's answer when I asked him if he thought the police would eventually get the killer.

"Depends on why they did it."

If Esmeralda is Ballero's niece, he would want to get the right person at all costs. Or would he?

Well, at least now I could go home to bed. Constanze Therese and her bottle of Cinar were no longer my problem.

21

I was driving in a blinding white mist. My headlights were of no use, reflecting back a dense wall of fog, making navigating up the mountain road even more unnerving. At least it was very early in the morning and there was no traffic. Occasionally, I glimpsed a single beam behind me and couldn't really tell if it was a car with a missing headlight or just a motorcycle. The driver had no intention of passing me, and after a few moments they fell so far behind that their light disappeared altogether and I was alone again in the clouds.

While it wasn't the most direct way to the Painted Cave area, I first went straight to the *Parque* and then followed the same route I'd taken with Dr. Lopez. I had to pull over every once and a while and walk on the edge of the road to check my surroundings. I'd almost reached the turnoff road when I noticed a red motorcycle emerging momentarily from the moving fog, almost immediately it was swallowed back into the opaque distance.

After what seemed forever, I found the spot where Lopez and I had parked his truck. When the door opened, Mostly took a flying leap from the passenger seat across my lap and immediately found a tree on which to lift his leg. I felt enormous relief as well, not to be driving anymore. I breathed in the damp air pungent with the scents of wet forest and relaxed into the muffled stillness. I took along a flashlight to help us find the trail and locked up the car. We headed out in the direction of the abandoned house.

The slippery gradient was difficult to negotiate, even in my hiking shoes, but Mostly managed it happily, digging his toenails in where I could only shift my weight into my heels. Again my thoughts went to how a body could have been carried up and out of this terrain, even in dry weather when the trail was in better condition. There had to be another path out of here, with an easier pitch, meeting the main road at another juncture.

Lopez had mentioned goat herders up here; surely, if I wandered around long enough, I could find a *Laurus azorica* tree near the meadows where the *Sabulosa* was discovered, and then from there I could look for some mini-cairns pointing me in the right direction to an alternate trail. I was carrying water and food in my backpack. Mimmo was still sleeping when I left home, but I wrote him a note explaining where I was, assuring him I would be back by siesta, and if not, to call Ballero. There was no reception up here, or I would have taken Mimmo's phone with me, but I had my GPS wristwatch, so I wasn't worried that we could get completely lost.

We found the house after a half an hour of scrambling down the incline. The mist was as dense if not worse than in the basin of the valley. The eerie silence, the dim light conditions, the deserted and decaying condition of the little house suddenly hit me in a big wave of fear. What had I been thinking? Why didn't I bring someone else with me? Mimmo would have certainly come if I had told him what I was planning on doing. Well, no, it was more likely he would have refused and insisted I leave this up to Ballero. Even Mostly seemed to be holding back, burying his head under his back left haunch and noisily licking himself.

We didn't have to go inside. That wasn't my job. My job was to find a habitat where the killing must have taken place. Ballero could search for evidence.

I stood there looking at the door. "Okay, boy, we're going in there, just for a minute." Mostly lay down on the ground and looked at me, his ears in the question mode.

"Come on, Mister Mostly, I am *not* going in there without you!" I said firmly, stepping up on to the dry-stone terrace. I lay down my flashlight for a minute and looked in my backpack for surgical gloves. I slipped them on, grabbed the flashlight again, holding it in my right hand while I pulled the old latch back on the door and then pushed it inwards.

It was cooler inside and a horrific stench hit us. I hung back on the threshold. Mostly ran through my legs to look around. In one corner of the room, a wooden table and three chairs with tattered, rush woven seats made up a primitive kitchen. An empty water bottle lay on its side on top of the table next to a broken dish cradling cigarette butts, wooden matchsticks, and bottle caps. I shone my light on the stone floors. My heart was pounding. I expected to see bloodstains, but all I saw was dust and a moving column of ants coming out from a crack in the wall in the kitchen.

Mostly scampered through to the back where another door led into what must have been the sleeping room. The smell was stronger in this room. In the gloom, I could make out a single bed in the corner. Mostly was already standing up on his hind legs, his front paws resting on the bed frame, his

146

nose poked into a big ripped hole in the side of the mattress, his short tail telegraphing his excitement, his fox-hunting Jack Russell ancestry revving him up to full-throttle. I pulled him off the hole, grabbing him by the collar, "Hey boy, let me see what you found."

I shone the light inside the cavity and saw the source of putrefaction, the remains of a large brown rat.

I gingerly pulled the rat out by his tail and laid him on the top of the stained, moldy mattress.

By his size, his small ears, and his hairless tail, I knew he was not your typical rat found living in conjunction with urban population. This was a wild rat, which normally lives underground in burrows, or in artificial burrows of his own making.

For some reason, the rat had chosen to make a nest for himself inside the fluffy cotton mattress stuffing material. Because I'd once had a Mongolian Desert gerbil for a pet, a species somewhere in the same evolutionary neighborhood as this *Rattus*, I knew that these creatures, too, take great oral pleasure in their ability to break down all kinds of materials with their needle-like teeth. They love building nests that they can continually adjust to modulate prevailing temperatures, shifting the material around and altering its insular properties.

I pulled out a 5X loop that I wore on a ribbon around my neck and got a closer look at his face and torso.

He had no obvious injuries and while his horrible smell told me he was several days into the decomposition process, because of his extremely dry burrow and protection from flies he still looked relatively good. It appeared that he'd died of natural causes—heart failure, or a stroke. But when I looked into his mouth, I became convinced he'd died by convulsive seizures. I took newspaper and a plastic bag out of my backpack and wrapped him up, then slipped the paper bundle into the plastic bag and back into my pack, under our lunch items.

I took out my dissecting kit and my largest pair of forceps. Sticking my hand with the forceps into the hole, I managed to get a good-sized clump of his nest. With the help of the flashlight and my magnifying loop I could see that, as I suspected, *Rattus mattress* had, indeed, woven strips of distinctly unnatural polyethylene confetti into the spun cotton stuffing. I placed my hand inside again, blindly feeling around, sweeping my fingers against the stuffing and the mattress lining. I felt nothing unusual. I withdrew my hand and looked closely at my latex fingers in the focused beam of light. I saw a faint coating of white dust. I tasted it tentatively with my tongue.

Poor Ratty, he had probably obsessively chewed on the plastic bags enclosing a couple of bricks of cocaine, then died within a few minutes of settling into his refurbished home, repeated trace ingestion of the crystals being more than enough to overdose him.

I smiled thinking of how surprised the drugs owner must have been at discovering the damage to their packages when they fished them out from their stash hole. They must have never noticed Ratty buried deeper within, which meant he hadn't begun to stink... which meant possibly ... I was lost in my thoughts when Mostly startled me by dragging something out from under the foot of the bed.

"Drop it!" I screamed at him, the sound of my own voice making me jump.

He cringed at my tone and released his tightly clenched jaws from the leather strap.

It was Esmeralda's purse.

I instantly recognized the knock-off Gucci bag I'd seen hanging off her shoulder, Friday morning at the fish truck.

Ballero was going to kill me. I hoped Mostly hadn't ruined his chance at prints.

I scooped up a confused Mostly in one arm and my backpack in the other. We had to get the hell out of there as fast as possible. I ran out into the bigger room and through the front door, stopping only to close it behind me. I jumped off the porch and started down the trail away from the house toward the valley below. I kept thinking I was hearing noises in the forest. Someone was following us.

22

Calm down, Epiphany, I said to myself, it's probably just heavy wet branches cracking, or birds thrashing around in the underbrush.

We stopped after a few minutes, and I sat down on a big rock to catch my breath, peeled off my gloves and stuffed them in my pocket. It was then that I realized I'd never looked closely at the top of the mattress, checking for bloodstains, I'd been so engrossed in Ratty and his hole.

I wasn't going back there, and I didn't need to. I just knew that Esmeralda had died in that miserable little room, and her body had lain there for some time—maybe on top of the rat's secret digs—before it was time for her killers to move it.

To help me calm down, I ate one of the sandwiches I'd brought along. Eating always helps me think properly. My grandmother used to say, "Bread brings your head back down from the clouds."

I'd promised Ballero I would call him as soon as I found anything. I'd certainly found *something*, it just wasn't what I'd been looking for. Should I take some more time to explore the valley, so that I could find the *Laurus* tree and maybe the trail where the killers carried the corpse back up to a vehicle? Or should I head back up the path, past the ghost house, to the place where my car was parked, and just get over to Lopez's office to call Ballero as quickly as possible?

My breathing had returned to normal, but I still felt edgy. I shared some of my water with Mostly. I couldn't shake the feeling that someone was watching us, but it was probably my guilt for playing detective in the house when what I was supposed to be doing was exploring the territory outside. I should have just insisted Ballero come straight up here with me. Okay, I was going back to my car and back to the *Parque* to call him.

I felt foolish, climbing back up the way I had just come down, and when we neared the house again I felt a ridiculous sense of fear and dread. I kept speaking out loud to Mostly as if that would normalize the situation. It took forever to get back up to the car and the fog wasn't any better than when we had left an hour earlier, no sign of sun burning through.

I started up the engine and headed back down the dirt switchback. By the time I found the paved road, I was deep in an imaginary conversation with Ballero, trying to develop a tactful strategy to get him to reveal his thinking on his only 'evidence' against Udo. Where was the dagger Udo had bought at Out of Africa? If Udo hadn't killed Esmeralda, which I knew was the case, whose dagger was it in her back? If there were only three, as Gaetano had claimed to Ballero, and one was bought by an elderly British collector months ago and one was still in Gaetano's shop, that could mean only one thing: Gaetano was lying or someone had stolen Udo's dagger to frame him.

If Ratty had died from raiding someone's cocaine stash, and Esmeralda had died in that room, presumably through her connection to the cocaine's owners, what could that connection be? I remembered Amy's saying on our last phone call, "Someone she didn't ..."

Didn't what? Didn't trust? You don't walk way into the bush with someone you don't trust. Someone she didn't what?

Someone she did not want be seen with! That could make sense. Someone she couldn't afford to be seen with in public, but someone she trusted enough, however mistakenly, to meet in an isolated place. Was she having a sexual relationship with someone that no one knew anything about?

I was lost in a train of questions, and when my attention returned to my driving, I became concerned that in the still prevalent fog I'd missed the turnoff to the road leading to the Parque. Instead, I found myself closer to the main road, which would eventually carry me back down into the outskirts of town.

I then made one of those fatal mistakes that sneak past the mind unnoticed, a moment of casually abandoned judgment. I decided to go back down to Ballero's office to tell him in person, instead of retracing my route back through the clouds to call him from Lopez's phone, as I'd originally intended.

Fifteen minutes down the hill, the fog began lifting and I became aware that I had to pee badly. I would have just squatted somewhere when Mostly and I were tramping around in the woods had I not been so distracted and nervous. I wondered if I could make it all the way to the police station without stopping. A few more kilometers of squirming in my seat and I remembered we were nearing the spot in the road where the Mirador perched in expensive splendor over the deep gorge below. It was still early in the day, but there might be someone inside already, cleaning, or doing prep work for the lunch meal. They would let me in to use the bathroom.

We eventually pulled into the empty parking area adjacent to the front gardens: a desert oasis of cacti and young palms laced with small rock pools, surrounded by a scattering of volcanic boulders.

I knocked on the massive wooden door at the front of the building. No answer. I looked around for any signs of transportation and found a motor scooter propped up on a side terrace with access to the kitchen. There must be at least one person there. I knocked again on the kitchen door, listening for sounds of activity inside, but there was nothing but an oppressive stillness everywhere. I shouted, *"Hola!"* to no avail. I guessed I was wrong about lunch. Maybe the Mirador only did dinner.

Next to the screen door, a garbage bin and several crates of empty beer bottles were lined up neatly against the outer wall of the kitchen. A low, wide perimeter wall girdled the stone terrace, overlooking the valley and the distant sea. I'd never had a chance to appreciate the vista from up here, as during my previous visits I'd only sat in the bar with Dr. Lopez. Once before on our trip, Mimmo and I had dined here one evening, but it was already dark.

Despite my pressing bladder, I picked up Mostly and peered out over the wall, looking westward toward the ocean horizon. Below us the sheer drop was dizzying. I took a step backwards and then Mostly began to growl. I whirled around and barely recognized Enzo, carrying a motorcycle helmet, coming up behind us with an urgent stride. Mostly's growl turned into an aggressive bark.

Something was wrong. Enzo was moving too quickly. He reached out and grabbed me by the shoulders. For a moment, I thought he was going to kiss me on both cheeks in typical European fashion, but why was Mostly barking like this and why was Enzo gripping me so hard?

In one horrifying second, I realized Enzo was pushing me backwards over the wall and at that same moment, Mostly flew out of my grasp, lunging for my attacker's bare throat. I remember Mostly's ears laying flat back on his head in ferocious anger, the surprise on Enzo's face. Then I was falling in space.

My grandmother would have said it was my guardian angel. But I believe it was all my years on horses as a child growing up in the foothills of the Santa Inez Mountains, those hours of wild stunt riding and practiced falls that saved me that morning in Spain. Somehow, at the last possible moment, I managed to hook my left arm over the edge of the wall while the rest of me dangled over a certain death. I swung my left leg against the rough volcanic rock face of the terrace overhang, desperately digging my toes in for the slightest indentation where I could temporarily press my weight.

With the aid of an astounding adrenaline rush, I twisted my torso, my right leg swinging back to gain momentum. The impossible strain on my left hand and arm was bad, but I got my right foot back up on the ledge, hauled the rest of my body up, and then rapidly somersaulted back down on to the terrace floor.

I was literally blind with terror. I had no idea where Enzo was. I rolled in the direction of the crates. In one quick seamless motion, I plucked out a bottle grasping it by the neck, and smashed its bottom against the wall, creating a crown of jagged glass.

I sat up. He was trying to get on his feet from where he must have tripped over a crate while struggling with Mostly.

He was trying to stem the fountain of blood that was squirting out from under a flap of flesh dangling above a dark hole in his neck. Where was Mostly?

Enzo was blocking my way out from the terrace to the parking lot.

I went towards him with my weapon, no thoughts in my head, only a white-hot primitive instinct informing every cell of my body. He curled up, raising his arms to protect his face and his wounded neck, pulling in his knees to guard the groin area. I plunged the bottle into a momentarily exposed strip of his stomach.

The heat of his blood spraying out onto my skin stunned me. I slowly backed off, the sound of his voice, groaning in pain, rocking me back into reality. *Oh God forgive me, God forgive me!*

I looked frantically around for Mostly, and saw his body crumpled in a corner of the terrace. I realized Enzo must have thrown him against the wall after tearing him off his jugular. Mostly's size and normally friendly demeanor disguised the powerful jaw muscles and scissor bite of his Jack Russell ancestry, and above all his fierce loyalty to me.

His muzzle and chest were stained red with Enzo's blood.

I was still afraid to turn my back on my attacker, but I squatted down to carefully gather my dog up against my chest. His eyes were closed and he was lifeless. I began crying.

I ran from the terrace carrying him toward the car. I held Mostly tightly in one arm as I frantically fished in the pocket of my pants for the car key. I got the door open and lay him down on the passenger seat. It was then I realized that I had pissed all over myself. My pants were soaked in urine and my right arm and shirt were splattered with Enzo's blood.

My hands were shaking so badly I couldn't get the key in the ignition. "Please, Mary, Mother of God, help me!" The motor turned over. I pulled out on to the road.

I sobbed the full twenty minutes it took to drive down to the Guardia Civil. I kept repeating "Mary, Mother of God" like a mantra. I drove on automatic pilot. Or maybe my guardian angel hadn't yet abandoned me.

It was a good thing that there was a vacant parking space in front of the building because I would have been completely incapable of parallel parking alongside the road. I got out of the car without bothering to shut the door behind me. Pushing through the entrance, I stumbled into the reception room.

I remember the officer in uniform behind his desk jumping straight out of his chair at the sight of me, a noise like the sound of the ocean in a seashell getting louder and louder in my ears, the room spinning. I heard a voice in the distance somewhere, tinny and mechanical, not my voice at all.

"I think I killed someone. Please help me, I've killed someone." Then the dark roaring wave pulled me under.

23

I woke up on something that looked like a bed but felt like a table, working hard to place the round leathery face peering down at me. A cloud lingered at the edge of my consciousness like a hangover coming in for the landing, but I hadn't been drinking. I knew that much.

I was wearing paper clothes.

The man smelled of cigar smoke and he was smiling at me.

"How are you feeling, Epiphany?" he asked in his gravelly voice.

"I don't know, really. Where am I? Have I been in an accident?"

His bushy grey eyebrows lifted quizzically. "I don't know, you tell me."

It was Ballero. What had happened? Why was he looking at me like that?

Nausea crept over me, as I gradually remembered the answer to my own question. The vision of blood shooting from Enzo's throat, and all the violence that followed was playing back in slow motion.

"I remember now. I was coming down the hill to tell you. I missed the turnoff to the Parque in the fog. I thought it would be faster to come and get you in person." I was speaking hesitantly as though I were reading from a monitor, but actually I was just trying to clear the fog in my head and convey clearly but without elaboration what I thought Ballero needed to know as quickly as possible.

"I stopped at the Mirador to use their bathroom, but no one was there yet, and I was on the side terrace by the kitchen, holding Mostly and looking over the valley at the view. He came up from behind me and pushed me over, but Mostly attacked him, and I caught the ledge with my arm and managed to pull myself back up. He killed Mostly, and then he was coming for me again. I grabbed a bottle and broke it, stabbed him in the stomach with it. Then I carried Mostly to the car and somehow I drove down the hill, but I can't remember anything else besides parking the car."

"*Who* are you talking about? *Who* attacked you? Listen Epiphany, I know you are in shock. The doctor doesn't want me questioning you for more than two minutes until you are feeling better. But if you have hurt someone we have to know about it. Maybe he's not dead yet. Your husband is here too. I called him and he's waiting outside with the doctor. Your dog's not dead either..."

I started to cry, surprising myself as well as Ballero. He reached over with his big paw of a hand and placed it on my head. "After you passed out, Luis called me and after we brought you to the emergency room, I went out to look at your car, and I found the little dog. We brought him into the hospital. He was only unconscious. One of the doctors here used to be an animal doctor. They have him in surgery now."

"*Muchas gracias,*" I sobbed. I could tell my blubbering was making Ballero uncomfortable.

"I'm going with my men up to the Mirador. *Who* exactly am I looking for? Was it the Russian? Did the Russian find you?"

For a moment I hesitated, trying to think who Ballero was talking about. Then it came to me he thought I had been attacked by the mafia killer.

"No, no it was Enzo. You know the Italian, Enzo?" Ballero was looking doubtful, confused. He pursed his thin lips together like he had bitten into a lemon. "A poor excuse for a man, but why would he want to *kill* you?"

"I think he must have been following me and he had something to do with Esmeralda's murder. I found her purse in a ghost house up there and I found something else as well. Where is my backpack?" I tried to sit up from the table and look around the room.

At that moment, the doctor came in, followed by a nurse carrying a glass of orange juice. The young doctor, who seemed to be not in the least intimidated by Ballero's status, told him in a firm tone that his visiting time was over. Ballero nodded in resignation, "I don't care how well she's feeling; she's not going anywhere until I get back here!" Ballero barked at the doctor as he walked past him to the door.

"Inspector," I called after him, "there's a dead rat in my backpack that will need an autopsy. I think he died of a cocaine overdose in the mattress where they killed Esmeralda. Get the rat to the vet who is working on

Mostly. Her murder had something to do with that cocaine and with Enzo. I'd bet my life on it!"

Ballero stopped in his tracks and looked back at me in exasperation.

"Frankly, young lady, your life is not worth that much at this point," and with that parting shot he disappeared.

I cooperated with the doctor's questions and examination. He explained to me that life threatening fear and severe emotional stress can cause loss of consciousness, but all the while we were talking, my mind was on Enzo. The nurse insisted that I drink the juice. It tasted wonderful, and all of a sudden I realized how good it was to be alive.

They listened to my heartbeat and took my blood pressure. It was only then that I felt the burning pain of my hand, and noticed how scraped up the skin was on the palm and on the inside of my arm. Someone had washed me clean of Enzo's blood and of my own urine while I'd been unconscious, but the raw exposed flesh on my arm was still weeping little droplets of clear plasmid fluid tinted pink with blood. Now the nurse dabbed at my wounds with a disinfectant that stung like hell. The pain-killing effect of my over-depleted adrenal glands was starting to wear off. I felt like a dried autumn leaf, all skeletal with broken edges. Everything hurt.

The doctor said my husband could come in for a few minutes, and after that they would move me to a room to wait for Ballero's return, as I was occupying one of their two emergency care beds.

When I saw Mimmo's face as he entered the room, I knew our marriage would never be the same again. I felt as if I were seeing him for the first time, a tall muscular man with glossy dark hair tucked behind his ears, intense brown eyes, and his whole being vibrating with passion and emotion. I was afraid of him. I felt words would never be enough. We could never really communicate.

I'd killed someone and had almost died. I needed him to put his arm around me and wait patiently. I needed him to trust me completely. I needed him to be calm and resolute, to give me room to tell my story at my own pace, maybe now, maybe tomorrow, maybe never. I didn't want the Italian tempest any more.

I put my wounded hand up, palm facing him. "I can't handle all your emotion, right now, please, give me some space."

"Space?" He looked like I'd thrown water in his face. The nurse tactfully followed the doctor out of the room.

"*Amore*, I don't even know what has happened." he pleaded, waving those ever-expressive hands in the air, his words tumbling over each other as he groped in English, Italian, and German, trying to express his frustration. "Ballero called me and said you fainted in the police station; you were covered in blood and Mostly may be dead. The doctor said he could tell me nothing but that you had a trauma and lost consciousness. Ballero wouldn't speak with me! He just rushed past me the hall ... what are you doing ... *what are you doing to us?"*

"What am I doing to us? What did you do to me Mimmo, that's my question! Who were you drinking with last night, Enzo? Were you and Enzo, maybe, drinking grappa, which we both know you can't drink without completely losing your head? And did maybe you happen to say something you shouldn't have to him? But why am I even asking you, as I'm sure you can't even remember what you said, as we both know when you get drunk on grappa you never remember what you did, or how you make a complete fool of yourself."

I saw clearly by the look in his eyes that I had hit the nail on the head.

"Well, I can tell you one thing. You might have thought Enzo was keeping right up there with you, but he wasn't, because he stayed sober enough to wait for me to leave the apartment early in the morning so he could follow and spy on me. Probably, just an hour or two after you got home from drinking with him. You know he can see our street from the balcony of *his* apartment. Well, he must've had a bit of coke to keep him awake too, a little coke and grappa buzz to get him up the mountain and down those trails."

Mimmo looked like he was going to protest but then thought better of it.

"And he followed me on his motorcycle all the way up to the Painted Cave road, and down the switchback, and it was so foggy, and he was so clever about it, I never saw or heard him. Well, I did hear him, but I thought I was imagining it. And when he saw me go in that little house that I found with Dr. Lopez, and where Enzo and whoever killed Esmeralda, yes—

that's where she died all right—he knew his game was up, and when I stopped at the Mirador, and he saw me standing so close to that wall around the terrace over that big drop, and there was no one around, he just rushed me and pushed me over. But Mostly attacked and went straight for his throat, and somehow, I caught myself! I went over but I got myself back up over the ledge, and then *I killed him*".

I paused to catch my breath and to really watch Mimmo's face while the news sunk in.

"I *stabbed* him with a broken bottle because I saw Mostly's body and I was afraid and I was in a rage and I was just out of my mind. And I don't know who I am any more. I don't even know that, and I certainly don't know what I feel about you, either, so just give me some space. Okay?"

I was shouting, crying and shaking again. I knew he probably didn't understand my whole tirade in English, but he got enough of it to be horrified.

He tried to put his arms around me but didn't speak.

I pushed him away. "Please, please, just go see how Mostly is doing. That's all I care about right now, and I can't go anywhere until Ballero gets back here. Maybe he's even going to arrest me."

"If you killed him, *it was self defense, Epiphany.* Please, listen to me, no one is going to blame you for that, not Ballero, not me, and certainly not God." His voice was firm, assured and emphatic. But he might as well have been calling to me from the end of a very long tunnel. I couldn't hear him. It was just an echo from a life I once knew.

24

Mostly pulled through his surgery in spite of miserable odds. His doctor told us he had a cracked skull, a broken collarbone, cracked ribs, and his right leg was broken in three places. When we first saw him it was a shock to see just how little there was left to look at. His head was wrapped in bandages with just his nose, mouth, and left eye visible. His upper body was in a plaster cast, and they had placed a preemie paper diaper on his bottom. Only three legs and his four-inch tail were free from plaster or plastic.

The surgeon gave us the address of a German vet in the center of town and told us he'd arranged for Mostly to stay there for post-op care until "we can place money on him," as he put it. He told us it would be some time before our dog would be able to recognize us or respond; he was still under the effect of anesthesia.

After he returned with his men from the Mirador, Ballero offered to drive the three of us to the animal clinic. He assessed that Mimmo, who'd arrived at the hospital by taxi hung over from his evening with Enzo and distressed by my story, was clearly in no shape to drive us there in my rental car. Mimmo carried Mostly gingerly as we climbed in to the roomy back seat of Ballero's Jeep.

Amazingly, the police had found little trace of Enzo except for a trail of blood leading from the Mirador terrace that ended abruptly in the front garden by a date palm tree. They speculated that somehow he'd managed to get back on his motorbike and drive away.

I was beginning to doubt my recollection of what had really transpired between us. Maybe he wasn't as injured as I'd assumed. The thought that maybe I wasn't a murderer filled me with such relief, it came like a shot of morphine coursing through my veins. I lay my head on Mimmo's shoulder, placing my hands over his as he gently cradled Mostly's head in his lap.

I had no idea what time of day it was.

It was growing dark and a storm was rolling in from the Atlantic. I was on the ocean side and fat raindrops peppered my arm through the Jeep's open window. The cafes and bars were pulling in their patio tables; shop owners dragging inside racks of clothing, handbags, and sunglasses displayed on the sidewalk.

Ballero's radio was tuned to the local pop station. We were navigating through the narrow winding streets to a reggae flavored hip-hop tune: *"Your body's banging out of control, ceiling to floor, only you can make me ask for more..."*

Ballero couldn't possibly have understood the English lyrics.

I felt as though I were high. I was alive and Mostly was going to live! Maybe even Enzo was alive somewhere as well!

I thought about that night he described to me working in one of Mother Teresa's hospitals in India after his wife died. We were drinking red wine in Fellini's backroom while Mimmo watched a Sergio Leone spaghetti western.

"I came to understand," Enzo had said, "that she *wasn't* a saint, not really."

I was shocked but intrigued. "Why not?"

"She *needed* all those wretched people with their terrible suffering. She was driven to them. She needed them and all that misery like I need to drink." He answered in Italian, and then added in English, "Whatever gets you through the night."

Enzo looked so handsome in the candlelight, his hair pulled off his broad forehead with a blue bandana, his grey-green eyes so sad and disarming, just another genuine mixed-up human being.

What had brought him to cross the line, to want someone dead so badly? Not just once, but twice. Well, three times if you counted my dog.

After dropping us at the German animal hospital, Ballero was heading over to Out of Africa to bring in Gaetano for questioning. The Guardia Civil had asked for my passport, which I thought was reasonable, as I'd confessed to killing someone even though no body had been found. They'd put out an all-points dragnet for both Enzo and Gaetano.

The Italians would not be able to leave the island, at least not on any of the ferry lines or from the private airport in the capital city. Ballero agreed with me that, at best, Gaetano had lied about the daggers to shift the blame from Enzo to Udo, and worse, maybe the ex-pro bicycle racer was Enzo's accomplice in the killing. One or both of them had enough knowledge of human anatomy to use that dagger with precision, and knew that terrain behind Painted Cave, knew the isolated ghost house and knew how to haul dead weight out of the *barranco*.

That person must have been Gaetano, not the wasted, slightly effeminate, 'Last Beach' denizen, Enzo. Gaetano had covered the island with his mountain bike many times; he knew the trails, the lay of the land. If Gaetano was doing some serious dealing, then hiding his merchandise distant from his apartment and legit business made sense. But what could have brought these two characters together in such a pact? We were getting closer. Yet at this point it was still a crazy, elaborate, and irrational crime.

The animal hospital was located in a two-story brick house, wedged in between a motorcycle rental yard and a German meat store selling *Vollkorn* bread and all the special sausages the local Germans couldn't live without. A blue and white painted sign read:

Dr. med. Wolfgang Fischer *Tierarzt/Veterinario Hablo Español*

Wolfgang Fischer inspired my complete confidence in his power to heal our fierce little Mostly. I saw the warmth and amusement in his eyes as I explained how my dog had defended me, and the consequent battering he'd undergone. The vet had long, straight, steel-grey hair streaked with white tied back in a ponytail at the nape of his neck, large gentle hands, and the slow, relaxed manner of someone who is fully present in every moment of his work.

Ballero waited patiently as the doctor completed his intake, gave us his assessment of Mostly's recovery, and explained in German that we could visit him in the morning when the hospital opened at 10:00. I then pulled the carefully packaged Ratty from my backpack and asked Dr. Fischer—in Spanish for Ballero's sake—if it was possible to determine whether he'd died from a cocaine overdose, as the rat had been found at what the police believed was the scene of Esmeralda's murder. This might be crucial to bringing her killers to justice. I showed Ballero and Fischer the sample of Ratty's nest material with its confetti of plastic bits woven in with the cotton fibers. I briefly explained my background, and why I thought that cocaine was responsible for the rat's death.

"Hair analysis," said the doctor, judiciously, "That gives the best result."

Ballero asked politely what that entailed.

"About one hundred milligrams of the rat's hairs," said the vet. "I can have my technician pluck them out tomorrow, and you can pick the sample up after noon, then send it on to a toxicology lab in Tenerife. The hair is dissolved with an enzyme, and then screened using antibodies that bind the drug in the digested hair. It's more accurate than urine samples, and anyway, it's a bit late to get a urine sample out of this little fellow."

Ballero laughed at the vet's joke.

I took a last look at Mostly, kissing his dry nose while Mimmo stroked one of his exposed legs. His one eye opened, but there were no other signs of movement.

"Don't worry, tomorrow he'll be better," Dr. Fischer assured us.

I knew Ballero was impatient to join the others looking for Gaetano, so we refused his offer to drop us off, saying we were perfectly capable of walking the short distance home, even though it was now raining steadily and a wild wind was howling outside.

We staggered down the deserted road strewn with trash from bins blown over, empty beer cans clattering and spinning down the cobblestone hill. I realized how drained of strength I was as I leaned on my husband's arm, my head bent against the stinging rain. I only wanted a hot shower, a cup of tea and my bed. But that was not to be.

25

We hadn't been back for more than ten minutes before there was an urgent knocking at the front door. Happy to be home, I'd just turned on all the burners on the electric stove in an attempt to heat up the living room, but the apartment seemed empty and cold without Mostly's presence. I couldn't imagine who was visiting us in this storm.

It could only be Ballero with more bad news.

Mimmo opened the door, and I was surprised to see a wet and bedraggled Serenella burst past him with a proprietary air. She was wearing a hoodie pulled up over her head, blue jeans and dirty, soaked, white Keds.

"Where have you been all day?" she demanded. "I looked for you *everywhere*, at the beach, the internet place, Fellini's, and I kept coming and checking the apartment, and ..." she was looking down the hall in the direction of our bedroom. *"Where's Mostly?"* Running down the hall, she called his name. "He's not here," said Mimmo going after her. "What's happened?" She almost screamed at us. I walked over to her and placed my hands on her bony little shoulders.

Looking directly into her stricken face glistening with rain under the overhead hall light, I realized she was not handling her mother's death as well as we all had thought or hoped for. I gave her a reassuring hug.

"It's okay. Mostly is okay. He's had an accident."

"What kind of an accident?" The tears were welling up over her lower eyelashes. Her lips quivered.

I guided her over to the sofa to sit down. In those intervening seconds, I decided to tell her the truth, the whole truth. I don't know why. Maybe I was just plain exhausted, and too tired to construct a plausible story that would protect her from the dark undertow that seemed to have us all in its grip.

I told her everything while Mimmo fixed us cups of hot, calming, *manzanilla* tea. I explained how my work with flies helped Ballero and the Guardia Civil find out the truth about where her mother was really killed, how Mostly found Esmeralda's Gucci bag in the ghost house, and how I suspected someone was following me in the *barranco*. When I got to the part about Mostly attacking Enzo, she smiled, tentatively. Her large grey eyes fixed wide open on mine as I told of stabbing Enzo with the broken bottle and running for the car with Mostly in my arms. I finished my story with the happy ending about the nice Doctor Fisher and how he was taking good care of Mostly.

"It can't be Enzo," she said simply when I was through talking. "You know Enzo?"

She nodded her head gravely. "He's a friend of my grandmother." Mimmo and I exchanged glances. "He is?"

Serenella was beginning to shiver. Mimmo went to get a towel and a blanket. I wished, not for the first time, that these Spanish holiday apartments would acknowledge the reality of cold weather and have some kind of heating system.

"He used to visit her some nights when my mother wasn't there. Late. I'd hear them drinking and laughing in the garden, and sometimes I saw him in the house too. He was always nice to me. He called me *'Mia Serenella La Bella'*.

I felt a stab of guilt, remembering Enzo's quirky charm. I found myself suddenly saying, "Well, maybe it wasn't Enzo. He had on a motorcycle helmet and it all happened so quickly."

What had Constanze Therese said to us the first time we met her? "I love Italians..." What did that really mean? What on earth had she and Enzo in common, besides drinking? Mimmo interrupted my thoughts, "Serenella, does Constanze Therese know you are down here with us?"

The little girl shook her head. "I don't think she noticed me leaving the house. She was watching television."

"We have to get you home, and I want to talk with your grandmother," I said hurriedly, taking hold of Serenella's hand and pulling her down the hall toward our bedroom, "Let's get something warm for you to wear."

I'd never felt so empty of any emotion except dread. I forced myself out into that fierce wind and heavy rain, to climb up those broad stone stairs to the big house. Mimmo had wanted to come with us, but I told him —in English, so Serenella couldn't understand me—that I wanted to talk alone with Constanze Therese because I thought she held the key to Esmeralda's death, and woman-to-woman I was going to get it out of her. Mimmo was too tired to argue with me. I carried the wet clothes in a plastic bag, and Serenella wore a t-shirt and sweater of mine under Mimmo's rain jacket. She shuffled beside me in dry socks and my high-tops that were several sizes too large for her feet. I shined my flashlight directly in front of her so she wouldn't trip in them.

As we approached the house, it occurred to me that less than twenty-four hours had passed since my last visit when I had found Constanze Therese so drunk, sitting under the avocado tree in the moonlit garden. It seemed incredible that so much had happened in the intervening hours. I wanted to ask Serenella if her grandmother had been drinking again, but I thought better of it. I'd find out soon enough.

Like strangers, we had to ring the bell on the formal front door because Serenella had forgotten to take her mobile phone or her key with her. Shuttered doors that rolled down from under the eaves closed off the open-air kitchen through which we normally entered. I was about to ring the bell a second time when the door finally opened.

I don't think Constanze Therese had even noticed her granddaughter was missing until that moment when she saw her huddling outside in the storm with me. She yanked Serenella inside by her left arm. I followed uninvited, and then she exploded in a dramatic tirade of such rapid and alcohol-fueled Sirenian Spanish, I could barely make out what exactly she was accusing Serenella of. Her declarations were punctuated with occasional indignant glares in my direction. The girl bent her head looking at the borrowed shoes, her hair hanging in protective curtains on either side of her face.

For the second time that long day, I discovered a lava-flow of anger pushing up through my normally composed surface. I took charge of the situation.

"Serenella, go take a hot bath, and then when you get into your pajamas, you can bring me back our clothes in a bag, okay? Meanwhile, I want to sit down and talk with your grandmother." She turned and ran back into the interior of the darkened house. I switched on a lamp in the sitting room to alleviate the depressing blue glow of the television, and so that I could really look into Constanze's eyes.

"Sit down Constanze Therese," I ordered. Her face was a study of arrogance and self-pity, a mixture that I find particularly unattractive.

"Her mother just *died*, and the last thing she needs right now is you blasting at her! She was worried about us because last night when you were extremely drunk—so maybe you don't remember—but I had promised her that Mostly and I would meet her this afternoon. We couldn't be there as I'd *promised* because your *friend*, the Italian, Enzo, tried to *kill* us. Mostly is close to death in an animal hospital right now, and I've spent a very long day in emergency care at the hospital and being questioned by the Guardia Civil. Do you know why Enzo tried to kill me, Constanze Therese? I thought maybe you might know?"

Even in my Mexican Spanish, Constanze Therese could read between the lines. Her eyes blinked repeatedly as she stared at me and pulled with her ringed fingers on the collar of her black sweater. With her other hand, she swept her dyed hair back from her lined forehead. I could see the calculator inside feverishly doing her sums.

"I don't know anything," she said stalling for time as she looked around for cigarettes. But I could tell the mention of Enzo had hit her like a grenade. I reached over the coffee table for the remote control and switched off the movie. She didn't offer me a cigarette or a drink. I plunged on anyway.

"He tried to throw me off the terrace of the Mirador, but Mostly turned on him to protect me, and I managed to catch the wall as I was falling. I had to kill him to save my life. I stabbed him in the stomach with a broken beer bottle." I felt as though I were reciting lines in a play, oddly displaced from the tragedy unfolding around me.

I caught the fear in her eyes despite the screen of smoke she exhaled.

"It's a *mortal* sin, Constanze Therese. You and I both know that the Church doesn't believe in relativism when it comes to killing. 'Thou shalt not kill.' Plain and simple. So here I am with a mortal sin on *my* soul because of something that was going on in *your* family, because I found Esmeralda on the beach. And today I found where she was *really* killed, but Enzo followed me, and he knew I was going to tell the police—and he was the killer, or one of her killers."

Constanze Therese was not as far gone as on the previous night, and though she remained silent, it was an alert stillness. Like an animal hoping to be overlooked by the predator.

"But I think, maybe this isn't news to you, is it, Constanze? That Enzo killed her. I think you must have strongly suspected it was him, but you couldn't tell Chief Inspector Ballero, *your own brother-in-law*, because then you'd have to reveal a family secret that only you and Esmeralda shared."

The older woman had torn her gaze away from mine, and was grinding her cigarette into the bottom of the glass ashtray with terrible intensity, as if she were trying to extinguish her own past.

I continued.

"I always thought it strange that someone would go to the trouble of bringing her body down from the mountain and arranging it on the beach. It kind of struck me like a mafia killing, like a warning or a vendetta or something. Of course, they were trying to pin it on poor Udo using that Tuareg dagger he'd bought from Gaetano's shop. And everyone here knows there is bad feeling between Udo and your family. But it was more than that, wasn't it? Your daughter was the victim, but he was really trying to hurt you. I haven't worked out Gaetano's reasons for being involved, something to do with the cocaine, but all this was mainly Enzo's craziness and it was something that was going on between you and him and Esmeralda."

I stopped to take a breath because I thought I heard Serenella coming back into the living room. But it turned out to be only the cat jumping from a table in the next room.

"He was a very lost soul ... an attractive guy for sure, but very screwed up by his wife's death. You don't think he killed her too? Then traveled around living off the insurance money?" My voice was soft and conspiratorial.

"He didn't kill her," she ultimately surrendered. "His wife. They'd only been married a few months. She drowned in a bad storm off Capri while they were sailing in a small boat. He blamed himself that he couldn't save her. He was almost dead himself when they found him floating on a piece of the boat."

"And then he got all that money so he never had to work again," I interjected.

"Yes, but he gave half of it away when he was in India. He ran out of money by the time he got to Sirena. She had been dead only two years and he'd gone through a fortune. He always called Sirena 'the Last Beach.'" She smiled a little ruefully.

My God, I thought. She's still in love with him even after he murdered her daughter. I remembered for a moment that terrible mattress where I suspected her body had lain. Ratty's hole and the powder traces.

"So he was an addict as well as an alcoholic?" I thought of his comment about Mother Teresa, *'Whatever gets you through the night.'*

"So, that's where you came in, you were supporting him here, supporting him in the style he was accustomed to. Do I have to ask why?"

I knew she would take the bait and defend herself in my eyes.

"We just fell in to the relationship naturally." She shrugged her shoulders defiantly. "He was renting one of my apartments and the day came when he couldn't pay the rent. I let it go for a while because I felt sorry for him. I knew his story by then, and he would visit to assure me that he'd eventually make it up. He always came at night and he was such good company. I was lonely after Esmeralda opened up the club. You wouldn't understand this, Epiphany, because you live in a very big world, but I live in a very small town on a small island. It doesn't matter that I have a lot of money. Everyone here knows me and no one knows me. Do you understand what I'm saying? It's a prison and when Enzo was with me I felt free to be myself..."

"And young again?"

"And that too..." She lit another cigarette and this time offered me one as well.

"Did you know he was an addict?" I was conscious that Serenella might join us at any time, and I wanted as much information as I could get out her before I went home.

"Not until we were fighting about it. He kept asking for more money and he was getting crazy. I only saw him late in the evenings, but I could tell he was getting very bad, he couldn't get an erection anymore. I don't know anything about drugs, but I could see something was really wrong with him and it wasn't just alcohol." She waved her hand for dramatic effect and I noticed her nails were lacquered bright red but chipped, as if she had been biting on them.

"So what happened? You cut off the money because of the cocaine?"

She didn't answer me. I could see how painful it was for her, but I could also see the visible relief in her body as she unburdened herself of the weight of her secrets.

"Not just that..." "What? What else was happening?"

"I can't tell you. I can't tell you that, Epiphany." She started to weep.

"Did you know Gaetano?" I switched my tactic and jumped to a safer piece of ground. "Why would he want to kill your daughter?"

She was wiping her nose with a tissue from a box on the coffee table. She shook her head to indicate 'no'.

"Well, I think he was the one who actually stabbed her, Constanze, not Enzo, if that's any consolation."

She balled the tissue up in her hands and pulled out another, getting ready for a fresh round of tears. "Where? Where did they kill her?" she whispered.

"In a ghost house up in the *barranco* near the Painted Cave road. I think Gaetano used Enzo to lure her up there. Obviously, there was no place down here he could have gotten at her without being seen or overheard. I think Enzo probably *did* want to get back at you for cutting him off from the money, but I think it had to be more than that. He wasn't just angry, he was afraid."

"Afraid? Afraid of what?"

"That *Gaetano* would cut him off, now that he no longer had any cash. Gaetano was his dealer. Gaetano owned him."

"But why would she go up there? Esmeralda would never go all the way up there..." Constanze Therese's voice was choked with frustration, as if by talking it out she could somehow reverse her daughter's fate.

Constanze's question was one I'd been working on for a long time, and tonight she herself had given me the clue to an answer.

"Did Esmeralda find out about Enzo and you, what was going on between you? Was she trying to stop it?" The expression of shame on her face told me everything.

"It was worse than that," she said weeping.

Then it hit me. I remembered Esmeralda's confession to the manicurist.

I'm becoming my mother.

"She was in love with him too?" I whispered incredulously. But I got no answer. At that moment, Serenella came back in her pajamas, carrying our clothes in a large blue plastic Ikea bag.

26

"Marriage is not what it's cracked up to be. You think that when something awful happens, the other person will be right beside you making everything better, but it's not like that."

I was indulging in an expensive therapy session using Mimmo's mobile phone. On the other end of the line, Amy made a sympathetic, monosyllabic sound but didn't interrupt my train of thought.

"It's like you get even more aware that you're trapped inside your own movie. Your husband is your co-star, but like you don't have the same director... or even the same script. The way Mimmo sees it, I didn't listen to his opinion about anything, and I was only interested in finding out what had happened."

"So what's his problem with that?" I could hear Amy rooting around in her refrigerator, looking for late night fulfillment. "I mean I understand why he was pissed about you not listening to him about the drug thing, but what exactly is wrong with wanting to find out the truth of what did or didn't happen to this poor girl? Or to his German hooker friend, for that matter?"

I was wrapped up in a spare blanket on the sofa in the living room, so I wouldn't wake Mimmo. I'd thought I was going to sleep for two days straight when I finally got to bed that night after my confrontation with Constanze Therese, but early in the morning I had woken up distraught from a nightmare.

Dawn was breaking over the harbor but it was still raining. Light bleeding through low-lying storm clouds was developing the view from our balcony in sluggish increments like a Polaroid photo.

I'd finally filled Amy in on the second autopsy on Dora—or "Strawberry Shortcake", as Amy had known her through my past phone calls regarding Mimmo's fall from grace in my eyes. But frankly, that drama had diminished considerably in the last twenty-four hours, obfuscated by the sickening reality that I'd possibly killed someone.

"Okay. According to him, knowing how and why Esmeralda died is not going to make the family feel better ... and I guess considering her mother's inadvertent role in the whole drama, he's not far off the mark."

"Yeah, but what about the concept of justice? Like making sure these guys don't kill again?" By 'guys' I think Amy was referring to Putin-face as well as the Italians.

"Well, he gets that of course, but his view is that these kind of people self-destruct quickly enough anyway, and in his opinion, if I really cared about preventing needless deaths in the world I'd be working on malaria, and not wasting my time with forensic entomology, which in his words is 'only an intellectual exercise'."

"*What?*" Amy's voice was vibrating with indignation. "Yeah, he actually said that the sin of Gluttony wasn't just about food and drink. He thinks it includes academics like us that are addicted to knowledge, stuffing ourselves with facts!"

"Epiphany, he's just really freaked out that you almost got yourself killed, and that Mostly is in such bad shape. I can't believe he really sees your scientific work as *sinful*. That's just too weird."

"But that's my point exactly, Amy, *I'm* the one who's suffering, and he's freaked out? I killed a man, or at least it seems I did, except we can't find the body. I just keep obsessively replaying those moments in my mind, questioning every microsecond. What was I thinking? Did I make a decision? Was I really convinced that I wasn't going to get away from him? You know what I was dreaming before I woke up tonight? I was dreaming I was Googling *'fatal stomach wounds'* to find out exactly what organs I punctured. He was bleeding so much from the throat and the stomach, I just don't see how he got on his bike and got out of there."

Amy interrupted me, "Honey, how long have I known you? Eight years? We lived like goddamn Siamese twins for three years, I'm telling you girl you did exactly what any sane person would've done. You're not a killer; there's not a mean bone in your body."

"Yeah, but he's right about something..."

"Who?"

"Mimmo... about forensic entomology... or anything forensic. He said that the state is only interested in people after they die, you know, like they will spend all this money to find out who killed somebody—but when they are alive they don't give a shit about them—they can go hungry or die of AIDS or lead completely wretched lives like Strawberry; but they can't be eliminated by someone else. *Because a killer is a threat to the prevailing order.* Only if you are a policeman or in the army can you kill someone."

"Goddamn, how did he get so cynical?"

I knew Amy well enough to understand this was not really a judgment about my husband. This was Amy trying to stick her pin in the map while keeping an eye on the moral compass.

"Speaking of which," I answered, "whatever happened at your trial, the pedophile...?"

"No verdict, yet. The jury is still sequestered." She spit it out. No emotional cadence, just staccato syllables as though she were relaying me information in Morse code.

"Well, I guess that's one case that doesn't deserve to be classified as an *intellectual exercise.*"

Amy made another small noise—a cross between a giggle and a yawn. We hung on the line together in comfortable silence. I shivered deeper into the blanket, beginning to feel drowsy. We'd been talking for over an hour. The chasm that had opened up between my husband and me didn't seem so drastic any more. I wanted to return to the warmth of the marriage bed, to the man who loves my dog as much as I do. I wanted to press the small of my back against his, the place where we fit together perfectly, mean bone against muscle, and sleep. I wanted to sleep.

27

People fall asleep when they bleed to death. They fall asleep and from sleep they lose consciousness completely, and then they die. The same as when people die from freezing to death. I learned this from Nunez when I called him at his office in Tenerife later that morning. I told him what had happened between Enzo and me, and how the Guardia Civil was holding my passport until they could find either Enzo or Gaetano and gather more evidence as to Esmeralda's death. I felt I had enough personal connection with Nunez that I could confess my mental torture about not knowing the outcome of my own impulsive act of violence.

Nunez knew the winding mountain road where the Mirador was situated; he'd driven it and remembered the landscape well. After listening to my recollection of Enzo's wounds, the pathologist gently told me that he would guess that Enzo had not managed to control his bike for more than ten minutes maximum, that he probably lost consciousness. Ballero and the police should surely be able to find his body and his bike somewhere at the bottom of the gorge. We discussed the unusually heavy rainfall and how that would make it more difficult to negotiate the terrain, but not impossible. I became depressed during our conversation as I realized the straw I'd grasped, after Ballero's initial failure to turn up Enzo's corpse, was only a construct of my own desperate imagination.

We discussed Ratty and the drug test the lab would be running with his hair sample. Without exposing Constanze Therese's secrets, I led Nunez to understand that the cocaine evidence would probably be crucial in tying Gaetano to the murder. Nunez then tried to assure me that even if Enzo's body was found, he seriously doubted that the Guardia Civil would criminally indict me. The pathologist told me that in his professional experience, Mostly's bite wound in Enzo's throat would satisfactorily support the finding of self-defense, along with the character testimonial that both he and Ballero would provide for me. He also pointed out that the Canary Islands' government is regionally autonomous, and that on some of the smaller islands such as La Sirena the state police ultimately held more authority than the Guardia Civil—Ballero's opinion would be the final word.

Mimmo was waiting for me in the juice bar down the street from the pay phone. We were having breakfast out. All pretensions at domesticity had broken down in the last 48 hours, and there was nothing left to eat in our kitchen. After breakfast we could go see Mostly and Dr. Fischer, then we had to take a taxi up to the hospital and collect the rental car we'd left behind.

I spotted Mimmo through the smoked glass doors streaked with raindrops alone at a table in the corner of the empty room. He was talking on his phone, and I could tell by the way he kept running his fingers through his hair that the conversation was winding him up. I went inside.

The waitress, leaning against the doorframe between the bar and the kitchen, was talking on her cell phone as well. The rapid vowels of their Italian and Spanish darting over each other were like small birds circling each other in the close, humid room. I sat down across from him, but the waitress ignored me, keeping up her spirited end of a conversation.

Mimmo snapped the phone shut and reached for his rumpled pack of Fortunas.

"What's wrong?" I asked.

He didn't answer at first. This was typical. The longer the silence, the worse the news was bound to be. I'd learned from experience he could not be prodded to divulge his problems. I went over to the counter and pointed to a pineapple arranged in a bowl of fruit and mimed a small bowl with my hands. The waitress nodded to indicate she would eventually get to me. I sat down again and waited.

"Gigi had a mild heart attack in the kitchen last night. They took him to Charité hospital and he's okay... but he can't work for a while. I've got to get back to Berlin, as fast as possible. I have to cook until we can get someone else."

Gigi was *La Strada's* hard-living but excellent chef. I wasn't at all surprised his daily habits had finally presented *la cuenta*.

"Nunez thinks Ballero might let me go. He thinks it's more his decision than anyone else's, but if they need more time, I guess I could stay on alone with Mostly until you can get back here."

"Are you crazy, Epiphany? I'm not leaving you here in this mess. If I have to call in favors, I'm getting us out of here tomorrow. *Basta!*"

"What did you have in mind? A call to Interpol?" I laughed at Mimmo's grandiosity. But it was true that in Germany, Mimmo was extremely well connected.

I knew Mimmo could probably get me out of trouble in Berlin, but I could hardly imagine a call from Chancellor Merkel would make a big impression on Ballero or the island contingent of the Guardia Civil... maybe Heidi Klum would work...

When the waitress finally made it over to our table, I ordered crepes and a double espresso to go with the pineapple. I was hoping a lot of coffee might act as a temporary painkiller. I felt like I'd been trampled by a herd of wild horses. An assortment of bruises in various shades and colors had appeared on my legs and arms, shoulders and buttocks. The acrylic nails on my left hand, which had dug in for life on the terrace wall, were now torn and broken, and the skin left on my palm was scraped raw and hurting. Maybe I could ask the kind Dr. Fischer for something to dull the smarting. But nothing was going to help soothe my tortured conscience.

And still there was this hunger to know more, the drive to understand the story, to trace the thread back to where the fabric of so many lives, including my own, first unraveled. Maybe Mimmo had been right about the compulsive distraction of the mind, the greediness of the intellect.

"How could Esmeralda have fallen for Enzo?" I asked him. "I just don't see it..."

"I can," Mimmo replied. "People are always creating their soul mate from the worst possible material."

"Yeah," I agreed quickly. "Just like God made Eve from Adam's rib."

"Think about it," Mimmo said, ignoring my joke. "Both of them had lost their spouses in even the same kind of accident—a boat accident. Probably some night, Esmeralda was closing bar and Enzo was crying into his drink and they told each other their love stories."

"And she saw herself in him," I suggested. "She couldn't have had any clue to what he was doing with her mother, or what a dysfunctional addict he was."

"He was intelligent and funny when he wasn't fucked up."

"Yeah, he did have his moments," I conceded. I knew that the ghost of Enzo's better self would forever haunt me.

"I wonder how she found out about her mother and him?"

Mimmo looked puzzled. "How do you know she knew about it?"

"Because of what Maria, the manicurist, told me. She said for the last month, Esmeralda was really agitated about something, and all she told her was that she was becoming like her mother."

Mimmo let go of the worry in his face for a minute and smiled. "For most women I've known that could mean anything including that she was getting fat."

"No, Mimmo, it meant that she found out her mother was having sex with Enzo and giving him money. I wonder if Serenella told her..."

"Epiphany, that little girl doesn't know what sex is, that I'm sure of."

"Yeah, but she could understand something unusual was going on in the house when Enzo came around so much. I just can't figure how Constanze Therese thought no one would realize what was going on."

"Or that Enzo himself wouldn't say something when he was really drunk," Mimmo added, "but I guess he was smart enough not to kill the chicken laying the golden eggs."

We dropped our speculations as the waitress came within hearing distance, carrying a plate of crepes and my coffee. As soon as she was gone, the phone began vibrating on the tabletop. Mimmo picked it up, *"Pronto."* He listened to the caller for a minute, all the while looking intensely into my eyes. In Spanish, he told the caller we were on our way to the animal clinic and then we would come as requested. I knew it was Ballero.

He hung up. "He wants you to give your story in a videotaped interview at Guardia Civil headquarters. They've caught Gaetano. Last night, he was picked up by the patrol craft of Customs Monitoring. He was around 20 nautical miles south of the island in an inflatable boat with two motors.

And they found cocaine on board as well."

"Where was he going?"

"Ballero didn't say, but obviously somewhere on the Saharan coast."

"How did he sound?"

"I wasn't there, Epiphany, how would I know?"

"No, I mean Ballero. How did he sound to you?"

Mimmo sat back against his chair and lit a cigarette, considering for a few seconds. "He sounded... excited and *allegra*." He made an arabesque in the air with his free hand.

"Well, I hope he's excited enough to give me back my passport so we can go home to Berlin."

28

The walls of the interview room were devoid of windows and painted a particularly disturbing shade of green. Combined with the fluorescent overhead light, it had an unflattering effect on Ballero's pigskin complexion. His colleague, Captain Medas, visiting from the Guardia Civil headquarters in San Carlos, appeared equally unhealthy. I found myself wondering if I, too, would look like a zombie on the videotape, recorded for posterity as an unattractive, distraught American woman, a not-so-accidental killer.

Captain Medas was apparently in charge of this phase of the case, as it had been under his direction that the patrolling Customs Monitoring craft had captured the fleeing Gaetano. The Captain's stiff and authoritarian posture was somewhat undermined by his pencil-line mustache and goatee, which told me that the person behind the uniform, like my husband, was approaching forty but still a follower of male fashion trends. He had light gray eyes that fixed on me as if I were the most important person in the world. This made me nervous, but at the same time Ballero treated me with such deference that it neutralized the Captain's intimidating manner.

I'd gotten to police headquarters by 11:00 that morning, after first stopping at the animal clinic, where I was reassured by Dr. Fischer that Mostly would live, and walk again. How much residual pain and restriction there would be depended on a dog physical therapist back in Berlin, whom Fischer recommended to us.

On arrival by taxi at the Guardia Civil, I'd been greeted by the avuncular expat British barrister, Dwight D'Antoine. Dwight was one of Mimmo's many drinking pals, and while I'd been visiting Mostly, Mimmo had hurried off on foot to Caleta—the town's hilly enclave of rich expat homes overlooking the sea —dragging Dwight away from his late breakfast, recruiting him on my behalf.

Dwight was overweight and overly tanned, like a turkey left in the oven too long, but endowed with a full head of shiny silver hair, which, I suspected, contributed as much to his confidence as did his healthy financial assets. Now he sat cozily next to me, facing off Ballero and

Medas across a diminutive interview table, as if we were expecting glasses of *vino rojo* and *platas de pulpas* to be set in front of us at any minute. His voice, with its upper-class confidence, had a bright promising ring, and I felt for the first time the faint stirring of optimism. Certainly, nothing bad could happen to me in the protection of such a splendid relic of the Old Order.

"As I understand it, Dr. Jerome has been helping you investigate this unfortunate killing and her recorded testimony here is purely voluntary."

I'd never heard Dwight speak Spanish, and I was momentarily taken aback by his command of it. He could actually roll off the elusive fluttering "th" sound of Castellano much better than I could.

Medas jumped in. "We have arrested a certain Italian store owner who we have sufficient evidence to believe was responsible for the killing of the nightclub owner." For one moment, I was shocked to realize that unlike Ballero and I, Medas had no previous connection to Esmeralda. To him, she was just a nightclub owner.

"As it may take an extended period of time to come to trial, and Dr. Jerome is a resident of Germany and travels often in her line of work, it is a precaution to tape her testimony. It may not be possible for her to return to the *Canarias* at any given date."

Suddenly, I understood Ballero and Medas were apparently not questioning me in regards to Enzo's death or injuries. Unless this was some elaborate poker game, they just wanted a record of everything I'd shared so far with Ballero that would help the prosecution convict Gaetano. I looked at Dwight conveying my doubts that it could really be so simple.

"I understood that Dr. Jerome has already written a report for the pathologist regarding the fly evidence."

"It's a bit more complicated than that," began Ballero, taking back the reins from the captain. "We haven't yet had time to go over the scene where the death actually took place. We know what Epiphany saw there and what she *believes* happened there, and we have found other evidence in the Italian's car parked near the San Carlos marina, where he rented the boat for his escape from the island. But as you know, yesterday Epiphany was attacked and treated in the hospital and was in no condition to lead us back into the *barranco* where the murder took place. With the storm, well, we are hoping that after this interview is over, she is prepared to do so."

The thought of returning to that dark little house made me shiver. I thought of the garish knockoff Gucci bag lying incongruously on the floor where Mostly had dropped it. "Of course I will, Chief Inspector," I said, "but what I want to know is why you haven't mentioned Enzo? *What's happened to him? Have you found his body?*"

I wanted to add: *am I being charged with manslaughter or what?* But I didn't need the slight pressure of Dwight's knee under the table against mine to swallow that last question. The other thought in my mind was: why were they in such a hurry to do this interview now, before we went up there?

"Can Señor D'Antoine accompany us into the *barranco* as well?" I knew that was asking a lot from Dwight, but if Ballero could huff and puff up and down those steep slopes, then so could he, and I wanted him with me—just in case there was more here than I could decipher at the present moment. I remembered Amy's wistful comment on the telephone, "Nice to have a rich husband..." I was sure Mimmo had offered to pay Dwight for his help, but I also suspected Dwight might be doing this simply as a friend—or even more likely—to alleviate the sheer boredom of retirement in paradise. The larger point was it was nice to have such a social and overprotective husband. Sometimes both of these qualities drove me crazy, but in this instance they were great. It would never have occurred to me *not* to come here and muddle through on my own.

Ballero cleared his throat. "Enzo's bike was discovered earlier this morning by some construction workers who are laying pipe for an aqueduct in the gorge," he paused, "but there was no body and, of course, because of the heavy rains there were no traces, no footsteps or anything to indicate where the body was taken."

"Where the body was taken?" I was completely confused. What the hell was he talking about? "Wild dogs," said Ballero simply.

"What?" I looked at Dwight and then back at Ballero in astonishment.

I knew that the Romans originally named theCanary Islands. According to Pliny, it was because of the packs of fierce wild dogs they found here that the island chain was called Canaria, namely from the Latin *canis* meaning dog. But somehow I was completely ignorant of the fact that these feral creatures still existed, at least on La Sirena. "You mean, all this time I've been hiking around, I could have been attacked by *wild dogs*?" I thought of poor Mostly and how I never could have defended him. He would have been lunch. It was good I hadn't known about them or I would never have enjoyed myself.

"Why didn't I ever read about them? Why didn't someone warn me?"

Ballero looked slightly embarrassed. "Epiphany, it's not like they overrun the island, but there are still some small packs left in lonely places. They use caves for their lairs and we assume that unless Enzo walked away from that crash over the gorge, which appears highly unlikely, what was left of his corpse was dragged away by a few dogs. If they had young...," his voice trailed away.

I was nauseated at the thought of it. But still I had to press on. "So you are not going to *look* for it... to be sure?" I felt the pressure of Dwight's knee against mine again.

"There are *many* caves here, as I understand," Dwight's soothing voice intervened. "Especially closer to the coast."

"Impossible!" Ballero wagged his round head in the negative emphatically. "We can't waste the men and the time. What's important is assembling the evidence to send the other Italian to prison for premeditated murder."

It was at that moment that I finally got it. They didn't care about the death of a drug-addicted foreigner who'd probably committed murder. No burial for *his* remains. No plastic flowers or holy cards for Enzo. Not even the Potter's grave that poor Dora Hoch would get if no one in Germany claimed her body.

What they cared about was nailing the one that was alive so they could have a public trial. The violence could be contained and displayed as the unfortunate aberration of a foreigner, with the result that business and tourism would continue as usual. And they certainly weren't interested in charging me with manslaughter or negligent homicide or anything else. They'd kept my passport only as insurance that Mimmo couldn't drag me away until they had gotten all the help they still needed from me.

I didn't know if I should feel relieved or what. I felt only the relentless persistence that one feels in a nightmare while the ego struggles to outrun a train, or swim backwards to escape sharks, that determined will to overcome the menacing forces of one's irrational surroundings. "Okay," I said, "But what about the other murder? Have you made any progress looking for the Russian?" I might have escaped one attempt on my life, but the memory of Strawberry's body lying like a discarded rag doll was still fighting for space in my nightmares.

"Turns out the German girl *was* registered at the Palma Canaria alone. She arrived that morning, but according to the passenger lists from the ferries, there were no Russians travelling," Ballero answered me.

This didn't surprise me. I knew all along that bastard was way too savvy to get caught. Despite Quill's scary warnings to me I wasn't worried for my own skin, I was too tired to be worried. I was more than bone-tired, I was soul tired. Really tired deep within. Numb.

But then Medas stunned me with his follow-up to Ballero's statement.

"Fortunately, we received news from our offices in Malaga that there was a raid there late last night, and twenty members of the Russian mafia were arrested on money laundering and racketeering charges. Including this man they call The Finger. It was a combined international law enforcement effort and my colleagues assured me this guy would finally be behind bars. In any case, if Dr. Nunez's lab can find the guy's DNA on the girl's body, we'll have him. If not, we probably can't pin it on him and he'll get away with it." Medas shook his head and stroked his well-clipped goatee. "These men have friends in high places in the Russian government so who knows?"

"Let's just get this interview over, so we can get up to the ghost house." I responded quickly, trying to be professional and cover the anger I was feeling at the world in general.

I looked Captain Medas straight in his light gray eyes. "Every living thing is food or eventually becomes food for another form of life. People like the Russian mobsters know this instinctively. They don't need a biologist to tell them. They just want to be the apex predator—the animal at the top of the line. But that's exactly what makes them so *morally* deficient. The motion of life, the transference of energy is not really a line—it's a complex web." My fingers traced an imaginary pattern on the top of our interview table.

"My area of study looks at how animal life decomposes and transfers energy to insects. Unfortunately, I knew too much about the fly that landed on Esmeralda's wound, so I couldn't just walk away and leave it to the police to find her killer. I thought I should help. My husband... he's Italian... he said I should stay out of it. He said Americans all think they can fix everything." All three men smiled slightly.

"Sometimes now I wish that I'd just listened to him."

29

"How much further?" Ballero's voice seethed with frustration at being left so far behind the other men.

I hung back behind with him to soften the embarrassment he must have felt watching Medas and the younger policemen gaining ground and navigating the slippery trail in relative ease, compared to his own breathless and tentative lurching down the trail.

The soft rain had finally stopped, and at this elevation the sun pierced the fog, cooking us in a steamy, muddy landscape littered with broken branches and slick layers of leaves blown off by the storm. For some reason known only to his gentlemanly self, the Chief Inspector was wearing his dress shoes, now not-so-shiny black cherry leather oxfords, which offered no grip at all. Periodically, I had to throw out my arm to catch him from pitching headfirst and rolling down the hill, wiping out the men hiking in single file below us like the remaining pins in a spare.

I was in better spirits, in my element, and relieved that the official videotaped interrogation was behind me. I wanted to give Ballero an excuse to rest and catch his breath. Thank god I'd had the wisdom to send Dwight packing after the interview, or I would have had my hands really full keeping both of them in vertical position. The English barrister had agreed with me that I was in no legal danger, and I asked him instead to find Mimmo and give him the news that I would be getting my passport as soon as I got through this last piece of police business.

Holding him at his elbow, I pressed Ballero gently back to indicate we should stop for a minute. "Chief Inspector, there's something that's been really bothering me, and I didn't want to ask you in the presence of Captain Medas."

Ballero raised his eyebrows and leaned gratefully against a tree.

"What made you believe Gaetano was telling you the truth about the three Tuareg daggers when you first went to his shop? It seems to me that he threw you off very easily ... and *whose* knife did they use to kill her?"

Ballero pondered for a minute. Then he spoke quietly and slowly. "Epiphany, I had no initial reason not to believe him. He was never known to us as anything other than a business man who paid his taxes like anyone else. I knew Esmeralda had some trouble—keeping dealers out of her place—but she never said anything about him particularly. The only bad thing I ever heard about him, which of course everyone knew, was that he'd retired from racing because he tested positive for doping after winning a Giro d' Italia some time ago. A man wanting so badly to win a title ... doesn't make him a drug dealer or a *killer*."

There was an awkward silence as we both realized that *I* would in all probability fall into the latter category.

"No, Inspector, but it does make him a liar, and I would think that might have occurred to you."

Ballero sighed. *"Claro*, in hindsight..."* He looked in the direction of the men below us. "We should catch up with the others."

"But did you find the dagger that Udo had bought from him at his apartment or was it missing?" I pressed on.

Ballero looked at me sheepishly, "He claims he never bought one. For all we know there could have been one knife, there could have been ten. It doesn't matter now, does it? What matters is finding the physical evidence to support what really happened down there." He nodded in the direction of the valley floor.

We began our descent once more. I showed Ballero how to sidestep his way down the path to make it easier on his legs. I was sure we were both worrying how he was going to make it back up again. "Look, I am sure there is another, easier way out of here," I reassured him, "they never got the body out of here on this trail that's for sure!" I threw my arm out again to steady him.

"When we get there," I said, "I don't want to go in that house again, so I'm going to continue looking around to try and find the other way out of here that they must have used. I think they could have balanced the corpse on Gaetano's bike and pushed it up... but there has to be a longer trail with a gentler ascent."

A momentary look of dismay passed over his face.

I remembered the dark mottling of pooled blood in Esmeralda's face, her stomach, her legs and the tops of her feet. The body had laid hours face down in the cool of the house, then wrapped in the plastic tarp —which, according to Medas, was found later in Gaetano's car. They must have set it head down, shoulders on the low, curved handlebars, her wide hips on the seat, the knife still in place.

Gaetano had wanted so badly to lay her out publicly on the beach, but why? Just to incriminate Udo, or was there more to it? It was a huge risk they had taken. Leaving it in the ghost house or out in the woods would have been the simplest thing to do.

Ballero seemed to be reading my thoughts. "Those crazy fucking Italians, what were they up to? Are they goddamn Mafia or what, those pigs?"

It was the first time I'd ever heard Ballero curse.

"What exactly do you know about the dealers in this town, Chief Inspector?"

As we made our way slowly but steadily down the grade, Ballero managed to fill me in on the history of what he referred to as the *plaga* on his town, his island.

I imagined Ballero to be in his late fifties, and to the men of his generation, the Lycra-wearing, tattooed and pierced hipsters were like locusts rendering the landscape unrecognizable overnight. The older people hated them. But what Ballero found most puzzling, he told me, was that drugs apparently appealed to an even wider range of people among the international tourists. Balding German accountants on holiday from their boring lives in Paderborn could be found snorting the white powder after drinking all night in the bars. Most of the dealers were small-time foreign punks making quick cash on vacation, but the local police and the Guardia Civil had recently noticed a more sustained availability. Ballero told me Medas suspected Gaetano had been supplying the capital city San Carlos as well.

"I went to Esmeralda and asked her. Everyone told me it had to be coming out of her place, with all the trash that went in there. But she swore to me she wouldn't have it. She told me she had hired that big bouncer of hers just to keep an eye on the trash and to toss them out. I believed her."

191

I smiled. "My husband believed her too. He said she always kept her own nose clean for Serenella's sake. But she would have told you if there was someone living here in town like Gaetano—whom she was keeping out of the club? She would have asked for your help, no?"

We were almost down to the level ground in the valley. Ballero was sweating profusely and repeatedly wiping his forehead with a white linen handkerchief, which he then delicately refolded and placed back into the breast pocket of his perfectly pressed shirt.

Before he could answer my question, I had a flash of intuition. "What if Gaetano decided the only way he would have access to the clientele at the disco was if he ran the place himself? Maybe he thought he could take over the lease from Constanze Therese if her daughter was dead. After such a horrible event, I can't imagine so many other people would be jumping in line to get the place."

Ballero pulled a pack of cigarettes from his pants pocket. He lit one, took a long drag and stared down at his ruined shoes, contemplating what I had just offered.

"Yes, I think she would have told me, but honestly, Epiphany, things were no good between us. For one thing there's a problem with the sisters, her mother and my wife. Hurt feelings that go a long way back. Secondly, Esmeralda always believed I was behind the people who tried to stop her making the nightclub. So she was very guarded with me."

I was astonished that Ballero was being so forthright with me. I thought with sadness how repressed family problems always have a way coming to light and the longer they fester, the more damage they cause in the end. I could imagine the 'hurt feelings' he was referring to might be directly related to Constanze Therese inheriting all the family fortune, and how she must have thrown her weight around in her younger days.

"Do you have any children?" I asked, suspecting I already knew the answer. He shook his head, this time wiping the back of his neck with the hankie. "My wife miscarried twice, and the Lord never blessed us with any more."

I'd seen his wife at the funeral. The opposite of the voluptuous Constanze Therese, she had a body and face that seemed to be all right angles and rigidity, but of course the relationship between form and function doesn't always apply when it comes to humans.

"I'm sorry. That must have been very hard. But it seems to me all the more reason you should try to get this sorted out with Constanze. I think Serenella could really use a grandfather in her life."

He nodded his head.

We remained silent companions the rest of the way down.

I parted with Ballero at the porch of the house and then continued down the valley in search of the native grasses where the *grillos* could be found. After a half hour of walking, I had long passed the spot where I had turned back with Mostly when I had heard mysterious sounds following us that foggy morning. Relying on my instincts, I started climbing again in an easterly direction. At one point, I came upon a spring forming small shallow pools with whirligig beetles skimming on the surface. I followed the spring water to its origin at a higher level of ground. The soil was less sandy there, and heavier with fungi and decaying wood. I remembered Lopez trying to conjure up the type of microhabitat where the *Laurus azorica* and the grasses might coincide.

I was getting closer.

I moved on a little farther and then I became aware of the high-pitched drone of male katydids. I walked toward the sound until it was pulsating all around me. I was on higher ground, in a clearing with no trees and no underbrush, just a quilt of faded, green-brown, waist-high grasses that I waded through, bit by bit, in the sullen heat. I became conscious of my breathing. I felt my heart racing. Just ahead of me, where the meadow edged on secondary forest, I saw a giant old *Laurus azorica* in full flower.

When I reached its cool penumbra my eyes adjusted from the dazzling midday sun. I initially saw just a blink of color. I moved deeper into the shadow, and then I recognized a pair of sandals. The left shoe was turned on its side, a gaudy strap of pink leather torn loose, tiny brown seedpods sticking to its Velcro tongue.

I imagined them taking a break from the heat, a pause in their grim labor. Leaning the bike against the trunk of the tree, laying the body on the ground. The weight of the head escapes the tarp momentarily, and turns slightly as the corpse touches earth, brushing ever so lightly but fatefully against the dried hull of a minute creature and a scattering of fallen blossoms. The shoes fall off when? After the last cigarette... as they shift the corpse back onto the bike and leave the shelter of the tree?

The katydids call. I step out again into the shimmering heat and look for the direction of the trail.

30

While Mimmo got our tickets at the ferry office for the next boat out from La Sirena, I took Serenella to *Uno Mundo* to get her an email account. I showed her how to send me a letter, and she chose the address: mostlyserenella@yahoo.es. I promised I'd write and send photos of Mostly and his recovery. I promised we would come back for another vacation, but I knew, even then, that I would never return.

I kept Constanze Therese's confidence, and when Ballero and the Guardia Civil presented their evidence to the Public Prosecutor, no one seemed to really concern himself with why Esmeralda went with Enzo down into the *barranco*. They were content with the DNA from the cigarette butts, the fingerprints on the beer bottles and her fake designer bag, the bloodstains on Ratty's mattress and with the cocaine traces in his hair sample and in his nesting material. Esmeralda's occupation as owner of the controversial disco was enough it seemed, to provide a logical link for murder. After all, this was still a place where they thought a picture of Christ sweating blood under a crown of thorns was an appropriate memorial for a young dead mother, not yet thirty.

I never saw Constanze Therese again. We gave the key to our apartment back to Serenella, who accompanied Ballero down to the docks to see us off at eight in the morning. Udo was waiting for us there as well, sitting on top of one of the tables outside the Once a Day. It was all very awkward, and Mimmo's hearty *ciaos* could not disguise our desperation to join the line of tourists making their way over the swaying gangway onto the boat.

Serenella cried and repeatedly hugged Mostly and me. Mimmo carried Mostly below into the lounge, but I stayed on deck, waving, as we pulled out into the open water. It was one of those rare days when the clouds from the rainforest drop down to sea level and envelop the coast in a shroud of fog. Within moments, their figures, one massive and portly, one lanky and tall, and the third, small and graceful, became indistinct and then disappeared completely.

* * *

Back in Berlin, Mimmo was swallowed up by the demands of the restaurant, and I spent a lot of time hanging out with Quill. We got drunk together one night after practice, and I broke down and told him about Enzo. He told me how he had killed someone, too, when he was nineteen in Vietnam.

The late spring is still indecisive, and sometimes Quill and I practice throws and catches in the rain, while Mostly watches from under the shelter of a bench in the park. My brave little dog hates limping along the mean streets of our neighborhood in Kreuzberg, his shaved parts exposed to the biting winds coming from the east.

I had to return right away to work at the museum, so I have been taking him with me every day, carrying him in a tote bag on the U-Bahn. He spends the day quietly under my desk in the small basement lab I share with three entomology grad students and a Plexiglas case of mice being raised for snake food. Occasionally, he shuffles over to watch the mice with interest, his tail signaling his repressed desires.

My supervisor and my colleagues think Mostly's 'car' accident was the reason I came back late to Berlin, and I can't bring myself to tell them anything about the murders or the true story behind my dog's injuries.

At the back of the museum, there's an abandoned wing of the building that was bombed in 1945, and because it was East Berlin, which lacked money after the war, the damage was never repaired. Eventually, the museum made income occasionally renting the back wing out as a location for war movies, and it was decided to leave it as is—one more reminder of what once happened here. Today in that blasted-out hollow, a small grove of saplings reach up from the earth, entwining their branches through blackened gridirons and broken floorboards that overhang in space. Since he doesn't like walks on the street or in the park anymore, I go there with Mostly twice a day so that he can relieve himself.

I've taken up smoking seriously. I smoke and he sniffs and wanders around in the weeds, while I look up through the ribs of this grand old building at a bowl of blue and unexpected sky.

Bonus Chapter: An exciting bonus chapter from the next Epiphany Jerome mystery . . .

The Girl in the Tower

A sultan had a much beloved daughter. One day, a seer in his palace prophesied that, on her 18th birthday, she would be killed by a venomous snake. The sultan attempted to thwart his daughter's early demise by placing her away from land so as to keep her safe from any snakes. He had a tower built in the middle of the Bosphorus where the little girl had to live until her 18th birthday. The princess was imprisoned in the tower with a maidservant, but was frequently visited by her father.

On the fatal birthday, the sultan brought her baskets of exotic sumptuous fruits as a gift, delighted that he had been able to prevent the prophecy. However, upon reaching into the basket, a small asp hiding amidst the fruit bit the young princess and she died in her father's arms, just as the oracle had predicted. The tower can still be seen today when crossing the great Bosphorus strait, which divides the Asian and European sides of Istanbul.

1

A waterlogged corpse is not easy to read, unless you understand aquatic insects. I am an entomologist and my particular expertise is insects that are necrophageous scavengers, those that eat decaying flesh. That is why the Berlin police called me in, and that is how I came to meet Arzu, the grieving, young Turkish mother, and how she came to tell me that God had told her that little Emel was dead by sending the stinging wasps.

I'm not sure about God, but I do know quite a bit about pain. In my opinion, if you can believe in God and that helps with your pain, then don't let me tell you otherwise.

Arzu told me she would always remember the wasps stinging her right hand, their ascent from the Amerikaner jellydonut, in the glass display case, to attack her so unexpectedly, as the beginning of her nightmare. It was as if Allah had sent her just a taste of pain to prepare her for the unimaginable torture that was to be her fate, once she learned, a few hours later, that her little Emel had disappeared only a few steps away from the family bakery.

Two weeks later the police recovered a tiny girl's body from the *Landwerkanal* which carries water from the River Spree through Kreuzberg: the immigrant borough of the city, high on population density and low on employment rates. The big question was how long had she been in there? Had such a small child really wandered off unnoticed until she had fallen in of her own accord, or had she been abducted and then disposed of some time, maybe even days later?

I got the call in my basement office at the Museum of Natural History at around five o'clock. As usual on a Friday afternoon I was alone, as the three entomology grad students in my lab always start their weekends before lunch. I wasn't exactly alone. There were also the mice in a plexiglass burrow of sawdust and cardboard toilet paper rolls. One of the grad students were raising them, sadly, to be fed at a later date to a South Ameri-

Laurie Taylor

can boa constrictor that resides somewhere else in this sprawling underground labyrinth of laboratories.

And there was Mostly, my small dog, who is allowed to accompany me to work, thanks to the uncharacteristic good will offered only to dogs by Berliners. When I first arrived here almost three years ago, to take a postdoc position in research at the Museum für Naturkunde, I was surprised to find dogs of all sizes and breeds riding buses and the underground trains, sometimes off leash, and sometimes even in restaurants and stores as well. Mostly is, morphologically-speaking, mostly Jack Russell Terrier, but polluted with "foreign blood" as the Jack Russell Terrier Club of America is wont to say. He amuses himself while I am working by following the antics of the doomed mice, sitting on a chair at a safe, out-of-reach distance from their terrarium.

It was five o'clock and I was staring out the narrow horizontal windows that overlook a courtyard. Because we're in the basement, the windows are at eye-level when we are sitting at our computers, so we can only see the feet and lower legs of people crossing to and from the side parking area.

I was wondering if it would rain soon, or if the brief but rapturously intense storms that frequently prelude our long balmy summer evenings would break later. I crooked my neck at a painful angle trying to assess the quality of light outside. Should I load Mostly in the basket of my bike and make a race for home before the skies opened up? Or should I settle in for another hour or two, on the trail of a new species of Simulidae breeding in the lotic waters of a lake in the East? The decision was made for me by the generic Nokia chime. No cheery hip-hop ring tones for me.

"Hey, Stretch, your services are urgently needed by Kripo." It was Quill Walsh. No one else used that nickname with me, and no one else I knew worked for the Berlin's Criminal Investigation Department, the *Kriminalpolizei*, known in short as 'Kripo'. Quill and I had become friends because we were the only Americans on the same city league fast pitch softball team, the Bones. He is our star pitcher and I play catcher. Quill is an outstanding athlete despite being over fifty *and* a pothead and beer drinker. He is a little slow running the bases, but he still got the MVP award at the end of our last season. The fact that he is some twenty years older than me, and that he has three kids at home, all from different mothers who ran out on him, keeps our relationship strictly platonic, but there was this chemistry between us, nevertheless. I admired him. He was still handsome and tearing away at life with all his teeth. We worked well with each other. Whatever the play, I always caught his throws and made the tag.

Quill has lived in Germany since the end of the Vietnam war when he had been sent to an American hospital here to recover from his wounds. He married a German and stayed on, eventually becoming a crime scene photographer for the BKA. He came from a Brahmin Bostonian family that disinherited him when he was so plebeian as to actually volunteer for the Army. He never returned to the States, and he counted among his many friends in Berlin, people who lived on both sides of the street, in the street, and outside of the law. He was a real gem.

"Is it official? I asked, "Or is this just your idea?" Quill had pulled me in on a case before, convincing his superior, Inspector Dirk Weingold, that I could tell them how a neglected old lady had come to die being eaten alive by flies in a neglected apartment block in a neglected part of town, Marzahn. I was hoping that this time Weingold had requested me without any prompting from Quill.

"Straight from the horse's mouth." Quill's voice was low and gravelly from decades of alcohol and smoke abuse but there was also a gravitas weighing it down in this call, no trace of his usual ironic humor. "We're down on the canal under the Möckernbrücke bridge on the southern *Ufer,* right across from the Deutsche Post. Making a recovery from the water. It's a really little child and she's been in there a *very* long time. The *Leiche* is in bad shape. Doc Hässing took one look and said to Weingold, 'Get that bug lady from the Museum to go over the body before anyone else touches it.' So we're all waiting on you. Are you on your bike?"

It was about a fifteen-minute ride from the Museum on Invalidenstrasse over to the spot on the canal in Kreuzberg that he had described to me. I needed another ten to get my collecting kit and lock up the lab.

"How soon is it gonna rain do you think?" I replied. I was thinking how a heavy rain might possibly disturb the evidence I could pick up from the body, and I had a vision of myself trying to concentrate under thunder and lightening which make me very jumpy, to say the least.

"Don't worry. They're constructing a tent over her as we speak." His use of the pronoun 'her' suddenly hit me.

"How could you tell it was a girl?"

"The clothes. Pink. And there's still some metal clips, shaped like stars stuck in the hair." My heart felt a quick stab, thinking of the mother somewhere who had carefully placed them there.

"It's horrible all right," said Quill, who despite having seen and photo-graphed much worse was still, at the end of the day, a father.

"I'll get there as fast as I can." I said, already planning my bike route through the streets where I knew I could safely run the red lights.

Fifteen minutes later I was speeding on my route towards the bridge, my equipment in my saddlebags and Mostly riding in the front basket attached to my handlebars. I could tell by the way he squashed himself down that he was a bit nervous, as I was whipping around corners and through the pedestrian crossings.

The humidity was so dense I felt like I was pumping away underwater. The light before a summer storm here is a soft gray-green, as if you are in a deep lake, swimming through a shaft of subterranean sunlight. It makes the colored and white paint of the endlessly graffitied walls pop out like startling vibrant fish.

When I arrived at my destination, the red and white candy cane-striped crime scene tape was easy to see. It blocked off the entire bridge with its embellished wrought iron railings, as well as the street intersections on either side. But a group of Turkish teenagers from the neighborhood had managed to climb down the banks on the opposite side of the canal, in or-der to get a good view of what was obviously a big police event.

I was locking my bike—despite the heavy presence of law enforcement—when the heavens opened. Except for a few key players, most of the cops got back into their vans. The teenagers stayed put, pulling up their hoodies, if they were lucky to be wearing one. The girls were all wearing head cov-erings anyway. I tied Mostly to a metal street sign where he'd be out of the way but I could still see where he was. By the time I ducked under the tape, it was raining sheets of dark water. An underling tried to stop me and then pulled away when Weingold barked at him. He and Quill and the medical examiner were down on a spit of land formed by a second retain-ing wall against the original bank of the canal. A police boat was moored next to it and they had set up the recovery tent on this narrow strip of soil.

Weingold and Hässing greeted me formally despite the downpour, holding out there hands like Germans do in these work situations. I always wondered how Quill led his double-life, working within this long reaching arm of the German Establishment. I caught his bright blue eyes and we nodded wordlessly at each other. I told Weingold that it be a good idea if Quill worked inside the tent with me, photographing the exact positions and locations of any of the natural trace evidence I might find on the corpse before it was transported. I asked to be shown the exact spot in the water where the body had been found.

The Inspector explained to me in good but stiff English how a woman, walking her dog off leash, had followed it down the steep overgrown slope when she heard him barking at something in the water. On closer inspection, she noticed the pink clothes, the small head wedged in between the bank and the side brace of the second retaining wall. In hysterics, she called 112 with her mobile.

Following the daily weather report is a bit of a national obsession in this country, but in my job it is central to my work. I knew for a fact that this summer we had already received four fold as much rain as normal, and most of it had fallen within the past three weeks, so water levels in the River Spree and the *Landwerkanal* were unprecedentedly high; the flow moving with rare speed. From Quill's description of the body and my glimpse of the recovery spot, I could think only one thing. This child's tiny body had been submerged, caught on something and held under, or maybe *deliberately* submerged for some time. The heavy rains had set it free, and it had then surfaced, floated downstream, and snagged in the crevice of the uneven wall.

This meant for me as an entomologist that I could in all probability be presented with evidence from two distinct habitats: terrestrial and aquatic. It was likely the child's hair would contain minute soil insects as well as water dwelling ones. According to Weingold, shouting over the din of thunder and the rain falling on the metal railway bridge directly over us, the toddler's head had been jammed up against the earthen bank, when her shoeless right leg hooked under the cement overhang.

We climbed back up to where the body lay now, protected by a tent. The teens were leaving, the violence of the storm too much for them. Quill was already inside, taking photographs. I struggled out of my rain jacket and shoes into the paper jumpsuit and slippers provided for me, carefully lifted the flap of the rain door, shoved my backpack in ahead of myself, bent my head and stepped gingerly inside.

She was not easy to look at.

When a body is recovered from water there are only four questions that must be answered.

1. Did death occur prior to or after entry into the water? (i.e. was the victim alive or dead at the time of entry into the water?)
2. Is the cause of death drowning? If not, what is the cause of death?
3. Why did the victim enter the water?
4. Why was the victim unable to survive in the water?

In the case of the body that lay before us, the last question was obvious and could be eliminated. She was a toddler, alone and unable to swim.

But the other three questions remained to be answered. Even at that moment, as I bent over her, my latex fingers delicately pushing aside strands of hair from the livid skin of her raw bloated cheek, even at that moment the necessity to find those answers had started to rip apart a family and an entire community. In the short gaps between the deafening cracks of thunder, Quill and I could hear the hysterical shrieking of a female voice. Then came the deeper rumblings of male voices just outside the tent, raised voices —back and forth—in both German and Turkish.

Our eyes locked. "What the hell?"

News travels at the speed of light in this time of smartphones.

Quill had set aside his camera and was holding a large magnifying lens with a light for me as I scavenged through the child's hair. I had delicate tweezers in my right hand and was trying to lift something I had found stuck to one of the small metal barrettes. The tent flap suddenly opened and Inspector Weingold appeared, crouching down, oblivious that his raincoat was trailing in mud, not to mention his shoes. His straight brown hair was plastered down on his forehead, his gold wire glasses gleaming in the artificial tent light, the lenses fogged up. He appeared flustered and apologized to me in a mix of German and English, "*Entschuldigen Sie das Störung*, Dr. Jerome, but we could have the mother here." He glanced over at Quill. "It could be better if we may make the identification now."

Quill and I looked at each other.

"You musn't leave," said Weingold. "It will be only a moment." The three of us all looked down at the little bruised, swollen and misshapen face. The curtain of dark hair parted on either side by silver stars.

"I'm sorry." The Inspector said quietly, "I know this is difficult."

I nodded mutely.

Weingold withdrew from the tent entrance, and then a Turkish girl, in her late teens or early twenties, timidly poked her head through.

For as long as I live, I will never forget that girl's eyes. Having your hair all covered up with a headscarf is akin to putting a frame on a picture. Her eyes were blazing green with tears. Her dark winged eyebrows like hawks on the descent. She looked in terror at the bundle on the floor, then up at me, the other woman in the tent. Her hands flew to either side of her face; she looked straight into my eyes as if I could hold her, save her. Her mouth opened into the shape of an O.

And then came the wail.

She was young, but the sound that she made was ancient. It carried all the agony of human helplessness, and love, and utter defeat. I tried to lean forward to touch her, but two large male hands came through the flap, locked onto either side of her shoulders, and pulled her back out into the unceasing storm.

Quill put his hand on the back of my neck to steady me. He whispered in my ear. "Just look through the lens, darling. Don't think. Just look for the bugs and finish your job, and when we're done, we can go to the York and have a whiskey."

You can't put too much detail on a label. Don't trust anything to memory.

That was something I learned early on in my training. Every vial, every cup collecting floral or faunal evidence from a crime scene or recovery site should have as much information recorded on it as one can possibly attain at that moment, when you are in the thick of it. I was still a long way off from my date with Jack Daniels.

Everything I found on the corpse and accompanying soil and water samples from the bank area where it was found was preserved in alcohol solution, and duly noted in waterproof ink with the exact location, date and hour of collection.

Then there were all the forms that I had to fill out to protect the Chain of Custody. Sitting in a police van with me, Quill helped with the German translations, while Hässing and Weingold spent their time in the tent. The ecological evidence would travel back, along with Quill's photo equipment, to the lab at Kripo headquarters; but we were headed to the York, the nearest decent bar to the crime scene.

Acknowledgments

So many people helped me while I wrote and wrote and rewrote this book.

Some were professionals who shared their time most generously. Thank you to Tom Maddox who read my first draft and pointed me in the right direction for the second. Thank you to Stephanie Glencross at Jane Gregory who, after reading the initial manuscript (under another title), wrote me the kindest and most encouraging letter in the history of author rejections. Thank you to Dr. Adrienne Brundage who reviewed the final draft for accuracy in forensic entomology, and who inspired the character Amy, years ago when we were in graduate school together. Any errors that may remain are mine alone. Thank you to Conny Kawohl for her brilliant cover design.

Some were literary friends that pushed me along through three countries and just as many years: Kristin Fischer, Adrianne Seyer, Seda Sedar, Priscilla Be, Moreno Santilli, Gerard Walsh, Audrey Mei and Melissa Holroyd. Thank you for being there—for both the ups and the downs.

But most of all, I am indebted to Nancy Chappel, who held my hand through all the drafts, for her close reading, sensitive editing and skilled proofing. Not to mention, she always shared her best Scotch whiskey when it got very late.

About the Author

Laurie Taylor was born and raised in California. After studying English Literature at Mills College where she was a Watson Fellow, she worked as a journalist in the San Francisco Bay area while raising two daughters. A second career as a science illustrator led her to a MSc. in Biological Sciences and work as a field biologist specializing in entomology. A chance meeting in India while collecting insects brought her to Europe and a year spent researching at Berlin's Museum of Natural History, which figures in the background of the first and second Epiphany Jerome forensic mysteries. She has taught English in universities and colleges in both Germany and Turkey. She lives in a pre-war converted factory in Neukölln, the Turkish neighborhood of Berlin, and is currently finishing a biography of her father, Dwight Taylor, a Hollywood screenwriter and *bon vivant*.

She blogs about books and bugs at www.laurietaylorbooks.com

The Favor of a Review

Reviews, ratings and comments on Amazon, Facebook or blogs of your choice would be greatly appreciated. I will read all the reviews of my books and love to hear what readers have to say. If you have a moment, I'd be ever grateful for your time.

Thank you very much!

CPSIA information can be obtained at www.ICGtesting.com
Printed in the USA
LVOW11s2048250916

506141LV00003B/727/P